Pennies for the Piper

Pennies for the Piper

Susan McLean

Farrar · Straus · Giroux

New York

Copyright © 1981 by Susan H. McLean
All rights reserved
Printed in the United States of America
Published simultaneously in Canada by
McGraw-Hill Ryerson Ltd., Toronto
First printing, 1981
Designed by Nanette Stevenson
Library of Congress Cataloging in Publication Data
McLean, Susan H.
Pennies for the piper.
[1. Mothers and daughters—Fiction.   2. Death—Fiction]
I. Title.
PZ7.M4787Pe   1981   [Fic]   81-4073
ISBN 0-374-35791-9   AACR2

For
HILDUR B. *and* LOUIS H.

Pennies for the Piper

One

Franklin Avenue was faded, shabby where the inner city gave way to rooming houses by the night, the week, or the month, payment in advance, no questions asked. Vacant store fronts with cracked windows and double-chained doors were posted NO TRESPASSING, BEWARE OF DOG, though there was nothing there to steal or protect. The sidewalk was littered with empty beer cans and broken wine bottles. But the broken pavement yielded dandelions and these Victoria noticed as she hurried by.

School was out for the day. Stubs was coming over to see her box of bugs and she wanted to make sure that there was enough bread in the house to make him a peanut-butter sandwich. There usually was no food in his house and, if there was, no one to fix it.

Victoria lived in a second-floor front apartment in a smoky brick building. It had been a double town house in its better days, but those days were long past. There was a flight of a dozen blackened stairs from the street to the first floor. Victoria took them two at a time and knew that there were fourteen more to the second floor. She let herself into the apartment as quietly as she could because Mums would be resting, or maybe even asleep,

3

and Victoria didn't want to disturb her if she could help it—Mums needed all the rest she could get.

The door *would* stick! She gave it a kick and it burst open with a groan. Shooshing it, she hurried to the refrigerator to check on the bread supply. There was a good half loaf, plenty for both of them. She carefully shut the fridge and brushed her hair out of her face. It was brown, shoulder-length, straight and fine, cut in bangs across her forehead to keep it off her face, but that didn't help much, and even a rubber band would not hold it for long.

She looked around the room. Her eyes, deep brown and nearly round, seemed almost too large for her narrow face. There was, in their expression, something between wonder and a sigh that did not go away even when she smiled. She was slightly built and her jeans bagged at the knees.

A newspaper was scattered on the floor near their one soft chair. She frowned. That meant that Mums had been out. She didn't do that except on certain days and this wasn't one of them.

"Mums?" She walked wide around the newspaper and went into the bedroom. Her mother was lying on the bed. She was wearing her nice dress with the skinny blue stripes. She still had her good shoes on.

Mums smiled at her. She had a pretty smile, like a light going on in a dark room. At least that's the way Victoria described it to herself.

"Hi, Bicks. Did you have a good day at school?" The nickname had come from Victoria's efforts to pronounce her own name when she was very little and hadn't mastered all of the sounds. Her early best had been "Bicksia" and her dad had shortened it to Bicks.

"Oh, not too bad." She sat down on the edge of the bed.

Mums took her hand and pressed it gently. A pause. "I was out today."

4

"I know. The paper." Bicks waited for her to go on, guessing what took her out.

"I went downtown," said Mums, "to the bank."

"No!" said Victoria, in little more than a whisper. "It's not time yet! It's not!"

"No, Victoria. Not yet. But I wanted to get it done while I still feel strong. If I wait too long . . ." She stopped.

"Yes," said Bicks softly. "I understand." She looked down at her mother's hand, traced the tiny blue veins in it, trying not to cry. She'd known for a long time that this moment would come. She had even practiced facing up to it, but suddenly realized that maybe she hadn't practiced hard enough.

Mums had gone down to the bank and drawn out the life-insurance money they'd gotten when her dad had died. That money she had put into a savings account for Victoria's future. She had sent a cashier's check to the funeral home, to cover her last expenses, but the rest was made over to Aunt Millicent in trust for Victoria. Because Mums was dying, it couldn't wait.

Aunt Millicent was all right. In fact, she was the kind of person you met once and felt as if you'd known forever, she made you feel so comfortable. She lived in a real house with an upstairs and a downstairs, and chairs you could sit in and not worry where you'd end up. But when you wanted your mother, no one else would really do, no matter how fancy their chairs.

"I feel much better now that it's done," said Mums, "much better. It's a great worry off my mind." She looked up. "Bicks?"

Victoria mastered her face. She met Mum's eyes and smiled. A little crooked, but it *was* a smile. "Sure, Mums, I can see that. I'm glad you did it. Now you won't have to think about it anymore." But the smile wouldn't keep and Bicks changed the subject. "Can I get you anything? Or do you just want to rest a while?"

"Some coffee would be nice."

5

"Coffee? Sure thing! Would you like a peanut-butter sandwich, too?"

Mums laughed softly. "No, thanks. The peanut butter's yours."

Bicks kicked the newspaper aside and went to fill the teakettle in the kitchenette. Two cockroaches were in the sink. For a change the water was hot right away and she scalded them to death, laying them on the shelf above the stove to dry. She set the kettle to boil.

"Stubs is coming over to see my bugs," she called, as she opened the refrigerator to get out the bread. "Is that okay?"

Mums sighed. "It's fine, Victoria. But I can't imagine anyone wanting to see a boxful of dead cockroaches. Bad enough we have them . . ."

"And better to have them dead," said Victoria. "That way they can't make more." She had plans for that box. Secret plans.

The kettle boiled and she made a cup of instant decaffeinated coffee. After she carried it to her mother, she got out a plate, a glass, and a butter knife, and set them on the table. She'd just about finished making a peanut-butter sandwich when Stubs stuck his head in at the door.

"Oh, hi, Stubs. Just going to have some peanut butter. You have some, too."

"Well, I dunno . . ."

"You'd better. Because I got the peanut butter out already and it's not polite to eat in front of people."

"Oh, all right . . ."

"Better have some milk, too. Peanut butter sticks."

Stubs grinned. "Don't mind if I do."

Bicks got another glass and plate.

He and Victoria were both ten, but he was a year behind her in school because, until she came along, no one had ever cared whether he went to school or not. His real name was Steven but no one ever used it much. When he was noticed he was called

6

Stubs, either because he was short or because he was stubborn, or both. A certain amount of stubborn helped, especially if the going was hard. And it was. His mom called him a "mistake from the beginning," his dad wasn't around.

If he were an orphan, Victoria thought, then someone would have to worry about him. But when you were only miserable and half bad off, like Stubs, then no one paid attention to you unless you got into trouble. An orphan—the word alone brought sympathy. But with Stubs sympathy wouldn't suit. He had his pride, after all.

Bicks understood that. They were really a lot alike. Stubs had freckles, though, and Victoria didn't. He was shorter than she was by at least two inches, and there was an air of neglect about him that you could almost touch. It was not so much in his clothes, though they showed signs of wear, but in the set of his face. And his eyes, brown and slanted up at the corners, seemed to be continually warding off danger, except when he looked at Victoria. *She* was no threat to him. His cheeks should have been round but he was too thin for that. His hair, much like hers in color, fell, uncombed and ragged, to his collar.

"You'll choke!" Bicks exclaimed with real concern. She'd never seen anyone eat peanut butter that fast. He nearly *did* choke.

He swallowed hard and had some milk. "Sorry, Bicks," he said, "my stomach is in an awful hurry."

"What happened? Did you miss lunch?"

He looked embarrassed. "Yeah. Guess I did."

"But you've got tickets!"

"Yeah. Well. I lost mine."

"All of them?"

"Naw. Just today's."

"Stubs, you're not telling the truth." She always knew.

He looked away. "Good as lost."

"Stolen?"

7

"Yeah. They ganged up on me. Took me down and searched my pockets."

"Who?"

"Don't matter."

"Yes, it does! Then you know who to avoid!"

"Won't help." Stubs looked ruefully down at the smears on his plate. "They'll do it again."

Victoria made him another peanut-butter sandwich. "This one's for lunch," she said. "We've got *lots* of peanut butter."

An idea slowly formed as she watched him eat it. "They'll never do it again," she announced.

"Yeah?"

"No, they won't. I guarantee it."

"What do you have in mind?" He wasn't too sure he wanted to know. "I'm no fighter."

"I know that. Fighting's not the way. It never solves anything except who's the biggest bully on the block. Now, here's what I've got in mind . . ." She glanced toward the bedroom door, then leaned forward and whispered her plan. "It'll work, won't it?"

Stubs nodded enthusiastically. "But your collection . . ."

"Never mind my collection! There are lots more where they came from. Don't you worry about that! I've got a big matchbox you can keep them in when you don't need them. And a safety pin, too, so you can pin your lunch ticket inside your shirt cuff. Okay?"

Stubs grinned. "Okay."

"Then let's look them over and pick out the best ones." She lifted the front of the sofa bed and took out a yellow shoebox. "You know," she said, "there's *nothing* as disgusting as a cockroach! Except, maybe, a June bug caught in your hair."

Stubs agreed. "Too bad it's Friday."

"Why?"

" 'Cause I won't get to try it out until Monday."

8

"Tuesday. Monday's a holiday."

"Oh, that's right. Memorial Day. I got you a couple of jars."

"Oh, good! What kind?"

"A big pickle jar. And a brown one, not so big. Stuff you chalk your coffee with. You know. Makes it look like you put cream in it, only it's not."

"That makes five, then. That's enough. I have three myself." She took the lid off the shoebox. "There now, how's that for ugly?"

Stubs gasped in admiration. The box was more than half full of dead cockroaches. He reached in and stirred them around with his hand. A shuddery thrill ran up his arm. They were awful! "You'll really give me some for my pockets?"

"Of course I will! What are friends for but to share?" She got the matchbox. "Want to pick them one by one? Or would you rather scoop?"

He glanced at the clock ticking away on the arm of the sofa. "Better scoop. Mom gets off work early today and I haven't emptied the trash yet."

"What about Stace? Doesn't she ever do anything around the house?" Stacey was his older sister. She was nearly seventeen and had quit school.

"Stace? I didn't tell you. She ran off. Had a big row with Mom and ran away to get even, I guess. I keep hoping she'll come back, but she hasn't. She's been gone a couple of weeks and no one's heard anything."

"Oh, I'm sorry, Stubs. I didn't know." Stacey, at least, was always good to him. And when she worked at the fish-fry place, she always brought him something to eat when she got off work.

"It's okay. Maybe she's better off somewhere else. Mom doesn't care." He shut the matchbox carefully so he wouldn't damage the bugs. "You want to come over and get the jars?"

"Sure. I'll just look in on Mums."

9

She was sleeping. Victoria shook her head slightly and tried to put the worry away. Going downtown shouldn't have tired her that much. She unfolded the blanket at the foot of the bed and covered her with it. It was cool in the room. "Be back soon," she whispered.

Two

Stubs lived third floor back in a shabby building a few blocks away. When they got there his mother was already home, putting away groceries and humming. He quickly grabbed the trash and took it out while Victoria waited in the hall. His mom was in a rare mood and he didn't want to spoil it.

Stubs's mom was unpredictable. Every once in a while she would notice him and make up for all her neglect with kisses and new clothes and good food. And Stubs didn't mind; gave him something warm to remember the rest of the time when he was always in her way.

She made them some hot chocolate, loaded with sugar, and watched while they drank it. It was great for Stubs. He'd have a good weekend. But it was embarrassing to watch, and Victoria escaped with her jars as soon as she could.

She kicked a beer can down the alley, then stopped to pet Mrs. Edmund's cat. She had to be nice to that cat because Mrs. Edmund was going to let her cut all the lilacs she'd need. "Funny how things turn out," she said to the cat, "just when Stubs needed it the most."

She let herself in and stashed her jars behind the bathtub. Mums didn't approve. Well, no, that wasn't exactly it. Mums

11

said she didn't want her doing it, that it was no place for her to be. But there was something behind her words, the way she looked at Victoria, that made her think she felt differently about it, as if she was really proud of what Bicks did.

This would be the third time. They used to live near a big cemetery and Bicks had noticed, walking home from school the day after Memorial Day, that some of the graves had really grand flowers on them, but some had none at all. Especially the ones with little stones near the fence. So she'd scrounged some jars, begged lilacs from the neighbors who had them, and put flowers on the neglected graves. She felt good about it, as if she'd made a friend.

"Where've you been, Bicks?" her mother had asked.

"At the cemetery putting flowers where there aren't any."

Mums had frowned. "Where did you get them?" She didn't want Victoria picking other people's flowers.

"They were given to me."

"You know your father's not there," said Mums, meaning the cemetery.

"I know he's not. But maybe if I put flowers on someone else's grave, then someone will put flowers on his, thinking that his people are all too far away or there isn't anyone left to do it." Her father was buried in Fort Snelling National Cemetery and there was no way to get there without a car. They didn't own one.

Mums didn't say any more about it then, but she stood a long, quiet time at the window, watching the rain.

They had moved that next summer and Bicks had skipped lunch twice for bus fare. It was the only cemetery she knew. Mums was still working then, and Bicks had put lilacs there on a Saturday before the grand flowers arrived. This year would have to be the last time. Mums couldn't object. Just the same, Victoria made her plans quietly.

This time she'd saved her bus fare from the grocery money.

12

A penny here, a penny there. She'd been doing all the shopping since January, when Mums had collapsed after carrying a sack of groceries up the stairs; it had given Bicks an awful scare.

Stubs had talked about coming along to help carry the jars. Now he had the best excuse for not going. He had to stay home to be loved. He would pay dearly for it—he always did.

The fact was that he didn't have the courage to step inside the cemetery gate, though he was determined to try, for Victoria's sake.

She started supper. Hamburgers without salt because Mums wasn't supposed to have any. It made her swell up. She wondered how Stubs was doing, if he'd reached the groaning stage yet. His mom had bought a lot of food.

She looked in on her mother. Still asleep. The trip downtown must have really worn her out. Bicks chewed her knuckles and worried, wishing Mums would go to a doctor but knowing, if she did, he could offer little hope. Her heart was too badly damaged. Any surgery would be a terrible risk and, even then, would buy only a little time. Perhaps he could help her with the pain. She was in pain most of the time, now, though she rarely spoke of it. When it was sharp Bicks could see it in her face. Her lovely, too-thin face became hard and set with it and she had trouble breathing. But she didn't want any help if it came with no promises. "I might as well die as I am," she'd said, holding Victoria close to her aching heart. "It would be so much harder for you to hope for a cure that is not to be, that ends the same way. I love you too much to put you through that."

Victoria slumped into the chair and covered her face with her hands. Mums had made all the arrangements several months ago for her own burial and for what was to happen to Victoria after she was gone. Two or three times a year Aunt Millicent invited them to come down and live with her. She had a big house and was all alone, but Mums always made some excuse not to go.

13

It was, Bicks knew, partly because Aunt Millicent had been against their marriage—Mums and her daddy—because she thought they were too young, too inexperienced, to join their lives. And she'd wanted her brother to go to college, to improve his chances in the world. But his desires were not hers. He wanted a wife and family, a job to put food on the table. He was not interested in further education, though he wanted it for Victoria. Until Bicks was born, Aunt Millicent had been distant. Then she'd changed. She saw their happiness and the joy they had in Victoria and, loving her, too, came to accept her brother's choices. Still, widowed and ill, Mums couldn't bring herself to call on Aunt Millicent for help. It was as if the sting of her early disapproval had returned with Mums's loss.

Time was short now. Mums wanted to be buried here, next to her husband. It was simpler to stay where she was, though she didn't tell Millicent that. She said they would think about visiting her when school was out in the spring. School was nearly out now.

Bicks shook her head as if to throw off the thought of being all alone.

"When I don't answer you anymore, Victoria, you take the money and the check that's under my pillow, pin the check to your undershirt, go down to the bus depot, and use the money to buy a ticket to Dubuque."

Victoria started up out of the chair. "When I don't answer . . ."

She hurried to the bedroom. "Mums?"

"Yes, Bicks, what is it?" Her voice was low and weary.

A sigh of relief. "Oh, nothing. I just wondered when you'd like supper."

"Suppertime already?"

"Nearly six o'clock. Maybe you'd like it just where you are."

"No. I'll get up."

"Okay." She went to the kitchen to get the things for the table. She felt there was something wrong with her mother's

14

arrangements, but couldn't think what it was. When she'd asked about it, Mums had denied it. Everything was arranged. Was it? Was it really? It seemed too easy.

Two knives. Two forks. Bicks set the plates on the stove, ready to serve, and drew the two hard chairs up to the table. Mums appeared in the bedroom doorway.

During supper Victoria talked about school. Little things that had happened during the day. How fat Mrs. Edmund's cat was getting. How pretty the dandelions were in the alley.

When they went to seed, she and Stubs would wish on them. If you blew all the fluff off with one breath, you got your wish. Her wish was always the same, but she didn't mention it. The dandelions weren't ready yet.

She told about Stubs's wish last fall: to get an A in spelling. She'd nagged him about it because the only way that wish would come true was to memorize the words. He'd learned all the words and gotten that A, but he still thought it came from wishing on fluff. Mums laughed over that story, which was why Victoria told it. Laughter was good for her, for both of them; a little forgetting came with laughter.

Bicks lay awake a long time that night, listening to her mother's breathing. A deep breath, like a sigh, then several rapid, shallow breaths, then a pause. Sometimes so long that Victoria started up out of bed. The sigh again, and she lay back on the sofa bed, springs creaking. After a long while, Mums said, "Bicks?"

"Yes, Mums?"

"You aren't sleeping?"

"No."

"Want to talk?"

"Would it help?"

"It might."

Bicks got up and, wrapped in a light blanket, sat at the foot of her mother's bed. They talked, not about what lay before

15

them, but of the past. Of happier times, when Victoria was a very little girl and had two parents. Of the things she did to get attention and how proud they'd been the day she learned to walk. How her father and his sister, Millicent, would vie with each other for one of her smiles. Not that they were rare, but that they seemed such a reward.

Memories were like a warm blanket and soon Victoria was nodding. She went back to her own bed and slept. Mums was up and dressed and having her coffee when she woke. It was raining.

Rain on the lilacs. Mrs. Edmund said they kept better if you cut them in the rain, but Bicks wasn't so sure about that. At least she wouldn't have to worry about the cat getting under foot. He always stayed in when it rained. He didn't even like to wet his paws with the morning dew.

"Sleep well?" Mums asked. She smiled.

"Yes, I did," said Bicks, smiling back. "Like a rock." She got some orange juice out of the fridge. She noticed that Mums had put a row of cockroaches on the shelf for her. Morning was the best time for catching roaches in the sink, though what they found of interest in a clean sink was beyond Victoria's comprehension.

"Thanks, Mums," she said. And then, without thinking, "I gave some away yesterday . . ." She stopped.

"You did *what?*"

"Oh. Well. Stubs needed them for his pockets." As if that were explanation enough.

"He needed a pocketful of cockroaches?" Mums looked as if she hadn't heard right.

"Well, yes. What happened, you see, is some big guys took him down and sat on him, went through his pockets till they found his lunch ticket. They stole it and Stubs went hungry. So I thought if . . . Well, if you're going to steal from someone and the first thing you come up with is a handful of dead bugs,

16

you'd probably quit right there and forget about the whole thing."

"And he doesn't mind?"

"Mind what?"

"Going around with a pocketful of bugs."

"Oh, no. Not Stubs. He doesn't mind. He's tough. Except for cemeteries." Victoria could've strangled her mouth! It was really out of hand this morning.

"I washed the label off the pickle jar," said Mums quietly. Victoria nearly dropped her orange juice. "It'll look better that way. Is Stubs going with you?"

"No. He was planning to try, but his mom came home liking him yesterday, so he has to stay around while it lasts. Just as well, he couldn't do it anyway. Oh, he'd have tried. He really would've. But I can see that he gets the wimwams just *thinking* about it."

"Why? Cemeteries are pretty . . ."

"His mom. When he was just a kid, just big enough to understand, she was mad at him. She is, most of the time anyway. She said that she was going to take him to the cemetery and tie him to a stone and leave him there all night with the bats flying around and the ghosts of dead people rising up out of the ground, hating him for being there and not being dead like them."

"She didn't!"

"Oh, yes. She did it! But someone found him right afterward. There would have been trouble for her over that, but she started to cry over him. 'Oh, my poor baby!' she said. 'Who did this to you?' Stubs was too scared to say. Matter of fact, he didn't talk at all for a long time after that. She never did it again."

"How awful! I'd think he'd be better off someplace else."

"So do I, Mums. I told him that. But he says he's got to stay with her because she doesn't have anyone. Stacey ran away and

17

there's no one else left. He figures it's not him his mom doesn't like. She's just mad at the whole world for giving her a raw deal and she takes it out on him. And he likes her, too, you see. She's his mom."

Bicks finished her juice. "Doesn't seem fair," she said, staring intently into the empty glass. "She's so hard on Stubs and she'll likely be around for a hundred years . . ." Mums put her arms around her and held her tight. It helped.

"No, it doesn't seem fair, Bicks. But things are that way sometimes." She brushed Victoria's hair back and kissed her on the forehead.

"Anyway," said Bicks, "I wouldn't change places with Stubs for all the money in the world!"

Three

Victoria went up the alley for the lilacs. Mrs. Edmund waved from her window and, later, when the rain let up a little, gave her a perfectly awful cookie that she'd baked herself. The white and purple lilacs were dripping wet. Bicks cut what she needed, and then cut some for Mrs. Edmund.

"Being as my joints are so bad in this weather," she said, "I can't get out and cut the flowers when they're prime."

Victoria made her a big bouquet and noticed that she put them in a three-pound coffee can. If Mrs. Edmund did *that*, used a coffee can for flowers in her own house with all the doilies and fancy stuff she had, then maybe it wasn't so second-rate to use pickle jars and cans in the cemetery, where there weren't any doilies, Bicks thought. Not that doilies had such class, except maybe the ones stiffened with sugar.

The lilacs improved the air in Mrs. Edmund's house. It always smelled musty and shut up, as if no one really lived there. Bicks thanked her for the lilacs and escaped into the rain before she could produce another cookie.

When she got home she found Stubs sitting on the front steps. Not minding the rain, he was just sitting, staring at the

19

traffic in the street as if it weren't there. He was wearing a new jacket and had fresh scratches on his face. She could tell that he'd been crying, but he was quiet now, as if he'd used up all his tears. There was a small bundle on the step beside him.

Victoria, respecting the state he was in, sat down next to him and waited. She had to wait a long time.

"Where do you go," he said at last, "when no one wants you?" His voice was flat, lifeless, as if all the sounds that made him Stubs had been squeezed out of him.

Bicks had never seen him like this. Even the time he had told her about the cemetery, his voice had trembled, there had been terror in it, but not defeat; not the raw hopelessness she heard in it now.

"There's no place to call home now." A shaky sigh. "No place."

"What happened?" she asked, not looking at him.

He shook his head slowly. "Don't know. One minute things're just swell. Then something happened. She changed." He looked at Victoria. "Sudden-like." He shook his head again. "Don't know."

Bicks waited. "Something come over her. I saw it in her eyes. She screamed and yelled for me to get out, scratching at me like a tiger. Doesn't want me anymore. Doesn't want to ever see me again. She tried to choke me. I ran."

He sighed. Bicks could see marks on his neck. Serious marks. "I hid in the cellar behind the furnace where no one ever goes. Heard her yelling for a long time. Then it got real quiet and I came out. Up in the hall by our door, I saw my things. Just in a heap, like they'd been pitched there. Just tossed out like garbage."

"Stubs . . ." Victoria began.

"She doesn't hate me through and through," he went on, " 'cause she didn't take back the five dollars she gave me last night. Jacket, neither. She doesn't, Bicks. Just something came

20

over her. Something bad-awful." He shuddered. "So I bundled up the things in the hall, and I came over here. 'Cause I didn't know what else to do."

"Why don't you come on in, Stubs. We've got room for you." Victoria picked up his bundle and stood up. "Come on, Stubs," she urged, "being wet clear through isn't going to do you any good!"

"Doesn't matter. Nothing matters."

"Stubs," said Victoria sternly, "*you* matter! Now get up off that wet stoop and come on in!"

He stood up. "Look, Bicks, I can't stay with you. You have trouble enough of your own . . ."

"Well, you can't stay *here!* On a wet stoop in the rain! You'd get picked up for loitering, sure as anything! Come on upstairs and we'll think of something."

He took the bundle from her. "All right," he said.

She led the way and he followed, shuffling like a tired old man. Bicks felt so sorry for him that she found it hard to breathe right. She could have broken down and cried for the way he'd been treated. But you couldn't think and cry at the same time, and what they should do called for some fancy thinking.

Stacey. She'd take him in if she had a place. Stace had always taken his side against his mom. But they didn't know where to find her.

There was another brother and sister somewhere, but Stubs hadn't seen them in years. As soon as they were old enough, they'd gone as far away as they could.

His father? Stace might know. All Stubs knew about his father were the curses his mom had laid on his father's head. He didn't know whether he was tall, short, fat, thin, dark, or fair. He'd left home when Stubs was two, leaving no memories, bad or good.

21

And Stubs was too young to get a job. Besides, he had to go to school.

Bicks laid the bundle of lilacs on the floor and unlocked the door. "You had anything to eat?" she asked.

"No. I'm not hungry anyway."

"You'd better eat," she said. She picked up the flowers and went in, motioning him to silence.

"She sleeping?" he asked. "Maybe I'd better go away and come back some other time."

"Where'll you go?" she whispered. She got him to sit in the easy chair and told him to take off his wet jacket. She gave him a blanket to wrap up in. He was shivering.

Bicks filled the bathroom sink with water and put the lilacs in it to keep fresh, then looked in on Mums.

"Who's with you?" she asked.

"Stubs. He's got a bad problem."

"What happened?"

"His mom threw him out. Said she never wanted to see him again. Threw his clothes after him. He's been sitting out on the stoop in the rain for who knows how long."

Mums gasped.

"He's lucky to be here, though," Bicks went on, "because she tried to kill him first. You should see his face. And his neck. All bruised where she tried to choke him. He's grieving something awful. I told him to come on up. He could stay with us, at least till we find Stace. Only he says he can't, figuring he'd just be a burden. He's always been in somebody's way. Gets to be a habit, I guess. Anyway, he's all alone and scared . . ."

"Someone should know about this!" said Mums, interrupting. "Someone who could help him."

"We do," said Bicks. "Anyway, it wouldn't do any good to tell anyone else. She'd deny it. She's changeable. And they'd believe her because she's a grownup and he's just a kid. Like that time

22

she tied him up in the cemetery and pretended that someone else did it."

"I suppose you're right," said Mums. She shook her head. "Stubs," she called gently, "would you come here?"

After a minute Stubs appeared in the bedroom doorway, struggling with the blanket, looking woebegone, like a half-drowned cat.

Mums smiled her most comforting smile at him. Stubs felt it and looked up, the blanket forgotten for a moment. It brought fresh tears. Victoria's eyes stung a little, too.

"Stubs," she said, "you're going to stay here for a while, with Victoria and me, until we find Stacey." There was a firmness in her quiet voice that brooked no objection.

He nodded, his eyes fixed on her face. "I have five dollars," he said.

She smiled again. "Take care not to lose it," she said. Then, "Bicks, is that old mattress still down in the cellar?"

"I think so. Want me to go look? Should I bring it up?"

"Yes, if you find it. It'll need some airing."

"I'll help," said Stubs, following Victoria.

They went out and clattered down the stairs to the cellar. "It'll be just like camping out," said Bicks as they tugged the old mattress out of the dusty corner where it lay. They dragged it up the stairs and flopped it down against the far wall. It was a narrow mattress or it would not have fit. It was covered with grit and cobwebs, and one corner had been chewed by something. Bicks gave Stubs the broom and told him to sweep it off before she put a sheet on it.

"Don't make it up now," said Mums.

"Why not?"

"It needs to air. And you both need some lunch."

Bicks dropped the spare sheet and hurried to set the table.

"I can help, too," said Stubs, following.

23

Victoria laughed. "Better not," she said, "or we'll all get stuck in the kitchen and starve! Only one person can turn around in there at a time and you even have to do *that* carefully!"

"Oh," said Stubs, looking defeated.

"Tell you what," she said, "I'll hand things out and you set them around."

There was the problem of the chairs. They only had two. "You're company," said Victoria, "so you sit. And Mums fixed lunch, so she sits." But Stubs wouldn't buy it. They ended up sharing a chair. It worked out rather well since Victoria was left-handed and Stubs wasn't.

Bicks washed the dishes while Stubs swept the floor. They'd made an awful mess with the mattress. Mums went in to lie down. "To be out of harm's way," she said. Victoria knew better, but it was a game they played.

She wrung out the dishrag and hung it on the edge of the sink. "Stubs," she said, "I've got to go out."

"I'll go with you."

"You shouldn't," she said.

"I'll go." He was determined.

Victoria sighed. "You know where I'm going?"

"Yes."

"All right. But you stop at the gate. You don't go any farther than the gate."

"I'll go as far as you go," he said.

"The gate." She was firm.

Stubs shrugged. He put on his jacket. "Can I owe you for the bus? Till I get my five dollars changed?"

"Never mind," she said, "I've saved up two bus fares, in case you could come along. And a 'found' penny for luck. When you find a penny just lying on the ground, you're supposed to give it to someone. Then it's a lucky penny. So you see, you can't pay me back or I won't have any luck."

He couldn't talk away the logic of that, if there was any.

24

Bicks said it so fast he wasn't sure. She gave him the shopping bag that held the jars, and after she looked in on Mums, they set out for the bus stop. At her insistence, he put his five dollars in the box of dead roaches for safekeeping.

Four

A steady drizzle was washing the air. Victoria and Stubs sat on the bench at the corner to wait. A bus came by full and splashed them, not even slowing for the intersection.

"A day like this," said Bicks, "is worth a lot."

The light changed and the next bus stopped. They got on and sat in the sideways seats behind the driver so that they could watch the money go down as people dropped it into the box.

Stubs wanted to ask her what she meant about "a day like this," but he could see that she was thinking hard about something, so he waited.

"How are we going to let her know?" she asked, five stops later.

"Who? Stace?"

"Yes. How are we going to let her know how to find you without your mom knowing, too?"

"Oh." Stubs put his hands to his throat as if to protect it.

"There's got to be a way," said Victoria quickly, "got to be. All we have to do is think of it. That's all."

She looked at him sideways. A mountain of gloom hung over him, and here she was taking him to a place that terrified him just thinking about it. "I wish we had a secret code," she said.

26

"What good would that do?"

"Well. If we had a secret code and Stace knew about it, then we could write a message on the sidewalk and she'd see it and know where you are."

"Sure," he said, unconvinced, "if we had waterproof chalk, too."

"We'd have to wait until the rain lets up. It can't rain forever. I've got some chalk." She sighed. "But it's no good without a code."

"I used to put arrows," he said, "before I could write. So when she got home from school she'd know where to find me."

"You did *what?*" asked Bicks, excited.

"Put arrows." He stared at her. "Arrows. You know. First you draw a circle, then you put an arrow pointing the way, then another a ways along, and another and another, till you get to where you are and you draw a circle with an X in it to mark the spot. Didn't you ever do that?"

"No," said Victoria, "but that's *it*, Stubs! A perfect code! And simple, too. Your mom wouldn't follow it, would she?"

"Naw. That's just between Stace and me." Gloom again. "What if she forgot? What if she doesn't come and see it?"

"She will," said Bicks on borrowed confidence. "She's sure to. If only to see how you're doing. She'll come by when she figures your mom's at work. And she'll see the empty circle and the arrows and she'll remember it, all right! Oh, I wish it would stop raining!"

"Me, too, kid," said the bus driver. "Only fools drive in weather like this. Fools and me. I sure hope my relief's on time." He pulled in to the next stop, Lake Street, where the lines intersected. A uniformed driver waited in the bus shelter. "Good," he said, putting on his coat. He winked at Stubs. "Hope you find your girlfriend, though I think the one you got is just fine. So long!" He stepped out of the bus into the rain. They stared after him, speechless.

27

"He wouldn't *tell*, would he?" asked Stubs.

"Wouldn't know who to tell what," said Victoria. "Besides, he sits all day hearing pieces of people's conversations. It goes in one ear and out the other and doesn't mean a thing to him."

"You sure?"

"Of course I'm sure!"

They sat in silence the rest of the way.

Victoria nudged Stubs, rattling the jars. "Next corner," she said. "You want to pull the stopper?"

"Naw. You do it."

She noticed that his knuckles were white where he gripped the handles of the shopping bag. She shook her head, inwardly, and rang for the stop.

They stood on the corner and watched the bus pull away, trailing swirls of mist. St. Mary's Cemetery was kitty-corner across the street. Chain-link fence, stone gateposts, double wrought-iron gates, low ground near the street but rising beyond. The monuments seemed to rise with the land. Mausoleums stared down from the hilltop on the lesser stones below. Beyond them was a huge monument to Minneapolis policemen and firemen who had died in the line of duty. And way, way back, in the oldest part of the cemetery, was a large, bare space with a single cross in the middle of it with only two words carved in the stone: ORPHAN BOYS. Bicks always visited that one first, then went to the graves nearest the fence.

Stubs began to shake in fits and starts, fear washing over him in waves, as if he were standing in a surf against a rising wind. It was a physical struggle, and Bicks could actually see him brace himself against the next onslaught. He was no match for it, and he trembled so that Victoria was afraid he'd fall down.

"Let's walk on down the street," she said, pulling on his sleeve.

He looked at her, showing more white in his eyes than she'd

28

ever seen in anyone's eyes before. "Think I'm going to be sick," he whispered.

"We'll walk slowly," she said, urging him on. "There's a park down the street. It's got swings and a really nice pool, and a bathroom, in case you need it. Come on."

"By a cemetery?" he asked, appalled.

"They've got to put it somewhere. It's a nice park. And you can't see anything from the swings except the bushes and the tennis court."

Stubs began to move along beside her, jerkily, like a wind-up toy. "How do you know?"

"We lived around here for a while, but it got too expensive and we had to move."

"Oh."

"That was worth a lot all by itself. Because it was nicer living around here. No cockroaches either." She quickened her steps to hurry him past the place that sold grave markers.

He clanked along, barely keeping up. "What do you mean, worth a lot?" She'd said that before, about the day. "Bad things are worth nothing."

"No, they're worth a lot!" She spoke defensively. "It's like a trade. A bad thing that happens buys a good thing later on. Maybe not today. Maybe not tomorrow. But *someday*. At least that's the way I figure it. It makes me feel better when I get to thinking nothing's ever going to come right."

"And then?" Stubs asked.

"And then I tell myself it's just pennies for the piper. The only difference is that I've got to pay in advance. And then I remind myself that, one day, he'll play me the tune, the piper will, and it's going to be a grand one, because I'll have paid so much!"

"Who's the piper?"

"He isn't anyone real. Once something happened and Mums

29

said, 'Well, you have to pay the piper sometime.' I asked her what she meant. She told me it was just an old saying. You sing and dance to the piper's tune and have a good time, but afterward, you've got to pay him. I asked, 'Who's the piper?'

" 'No one,' she said. 'He's not a real person. It's just the notion that you pay for all of your good times.' And then she changed the subject."

They cut across the tennis courts. "I got to thinking about that and I figured if you had to pay afterward, how come it seems like you pay and pay and don't get anything for it? That's when I figured that I was paying my dues for good things later on. Sometimes it takes *some* believing!"

"Going to the cemetery," Stubs asked, "is *that* paying?"

"No, because it doesn't worry me. It's just something I do."

"If I was to go to the cemetery?" he asked.

"It'd be worth a lot. But you can't do it. You know that, now. It's nothing to be ashamed of. It's just the way things are."

They reached the play area. "Looks like you've got it all to yourself," she said. "Now you wait for me here. I'll be back in a little while." She took the shopping bag from him. "Won't take long."

"Where'll you be?"

"Near the fence. You can see it from the street." She would hurry with the orphans. If he did get his courage up, she knew that would be too great a distance for his strength.

There were puddles under all the swings, but Stubs's shoes were so wet that it didn't matter. He got on a swing. Victoria looked back once, as she walked away, to see him swinging slowly and solemnly. Like a funeral bell, she thought. He stared fixedly at the wet bushes in front of him that shielded his eyes from his terror.

Bicks entered the cemetery through a narrow gate and felt the green quiet of it surround her. So different from the hard, treeless place where she lived. And she knew that when

30

Mums . . . when Mums . . . Well, it would be in a place *like* this with grass and trees and peace. She'd been there for her father's funeral. She knew.

She hurried along the winding road to where the orphan boys were laid to rest. There were no names or dates; who would come if she didn't?

A robin sauced at her for disturbing his meal and a squirrel scolded, shaking rain from a tree. Bicks filled a jar with water from the standpipe at the edge of the road and set it down carefully in front of the cross. She put a bigger share of lilacs on this plot, for these graves, because there was no one else to come. She hurried back to the fence. The grand flowers still hadn't arrived.

She filled another jar and worked her way along the fence. She selected a gravestone by how far the grass had grown over it, and she got out her scissors to trim the grass away. "A long time ago," she said. "Bet that you haven't got anyone left."

She set the jar on the stone, between the dates, and put some of the lilacs in it, fluffing them to look like more. The next one had a headstone, which put it in the fancy category, but it was so old she was sure it would be neglected.

She was working her way toward the main gates now. The coffee can right up against the fence because it was biggest and had to do for six. The dates on one of the stones were only two years apart—a baby in a full-sized grave.

"Bicks?" A choked whisper. She looked up to see Stubs. "It's all right," he said, "I already threw up. I want to help." His face was bleached white and there were livid spots on his cheeks, but he wasn't trembling. She handed him the scissors and told him how to trim around the stones. It looked odd to see him using his right hand, but the scissors cut better that way.

"Why do you do this?" he asked.

"It makes it look neater. As if somebody cared," she said. She kept talking. Talk could hold back fear better than whistling in

31

the dark. Stubs had come so far alone, she didn't want him to back off and bolt. "It goes one better than the ones with the grand flowers, because that's all they get, a bunch of fancy flowers. They call up and order them and someone comes out in a truck and puts them there, not even bothering to clear the grass away from the markers because they've got a lot of deliveries to make and all the rich folks pay for are the flowers. So maybe it looks more like we care. And what if, one day, someone comes who's related to one of ours, and they look at the stone, all trim and neat. It would make them feel better to see that, even if they can't come so very often, someone's been there before them. And they go away feeling good about it. See?"

"Yeah," said Stubs, "I see. And it makes *you* feel good, too, doesn't it?" His voice was a little stronger, as if he was finding it again.

Only one more to go. They moved on. "Sure it does."

Stubs trimmed around the stone while Victoria went to fill the jar with water. When she came back, he looked up at her too quickly and she saw the relief he tried to hide.

"I don't think we can get all these flowers in," she said, as she set the brown jar on the stone.

"Squeeze them," said Stubs, watching.

"I did that once," she said. "Broke the jar and nearly cut myself." Jiggling and shoving, she got all but one of the branches in. "Let's take this one home to Mums, she likes lilacs."

"Wouldn't she mind? Same ones we took to the cemetery and all?"

"Oh. But what'll we do with it?"

Stubs picked up the branch. "Share it out," he said. He clipped off all the flower clusters and carefully stuck one cluster into the ground by each of the last five stones next to the gate, dropping the stripped branch into the wire trash basket.

Bicks watched him. It was a nice gesture, though she knew the flowers wouldn't last long. And neither would he. His hands

32

had begun to shake again, and a sudden shudder ran across his shoulders as he discarded the branch.

She hurried him out the gate. "Do you want to wait here for the bus?" she asked. There was an iron bench at the corner outside the cemetery. "Or would you rather walk up to the next corner?"

"You choose," he said. He'd made all the decisions he could for that day.

"Okay," said Victoria, carefully folding the shopping bag. It was a good one, made of heavy plastic with sturdy handles. She stepped off the curb into the street and looked to see if a bus was coming. "Let's wait here," she said. "I think I see one a couple of blocks away. If not, then we'll walk up to the next corner."

Stubs nodded, beyond speech.

The bus came and they got on. It was good to be out of the rain and even better, for Stubs, to be moving rapidly away from the cemetery. Neither of them spoke until they got off at the corner near Victoria's house.

"That was the bravest thing I've even seen anyone do," said Bicks.

"For the piper," he mumbled, "it's worth a *lot*."

33

Five

Safely inside the little apartment, Victoria became brisk and bossy. She made Stubs take a hot bath, "for the chill," she said, and made up the mattress on the floor. One sheet was all they had to spare. The blanket was faded but warm and it had no big holes in it. She laid it on to its best advantage and put her own pillow on the top.

Stubs emerged from the bathroom meek and still shivering. He wore an old shirt and trousers. He had no pajamas. Bicks bossed him into bed, telling him he'd done enough for one day, and anyway, he'd have to stay there until he got warm. She made him some hot chocolate from a package and he went right to sleep.

"Victoria?" Mums called.

"Yes, Mums?" asked Bicks, looking in on her.

She smiled. "Now that you've taken care of Stubs," she said, "you'd better see to yourself."

"Just about to," said Bicks, but she didn't right away. She sat on the end of the bed and told Mums about Stubs and how brave he'd been.

"Maybe he felt he *had* to help," said Mums.

34

"No, that wasn't it," said Victoria. "He didn't even have to come along. I wish he hadn't."

"Why?"

"Because he's been through enough already."

"It breaks my heart to see him," said Mums. She took Victoria's hand and squeezed it. "We'll take good care of him to make up for today. Now, you scoot and get into some dry clothes! Then we'll talk about supper."

Bicks changed clothes, then strung a line back and forth across the bathroom and hung up all their wet things. She took the remains of Stubs's bundle and folded what clothes there were, making a neat pile at the foot of his bed, the matchbox on top. There was his toothbrush and, for some reason, a bar of soap in its wrapper. At least his mom had been thorough—go away but don't forget to wash behind your ears. She put it in the bathroom.

Stubs cried out in his sleep and then he screamed, "Momma, don't!" He sat up, eyes wide but unseeing. "Don't hurt me!" he begged.

Bicks hurried toward him, but Mums was already there, kneeling by his side, gasping for breath. She laid him down gently, then held him there for a minute or two, waiting to catch her breath, waiting till he stopped screaming.

She spoke softly then, rubbing his back with her fingers. "It's all right, Stubs," she said. "It's all right. You're safe here. No one's going to hurt you. It's all right."

After a little while the nightmare passed and he fell, once more, into a deep sleep. Victoria helped her mother to her feet. She was weeping at Stubs's anguish.

"I'll sit in the chair for a while," said Mums.

"All right," said Bicks. She knew that sitting up sometimes eased the pain. She shouldn't have done that, moved so quickly to Stubs's side. But she couldn't help it. She was a mother and Stubs needed comfort.

35

He woke toward evening and sat up, looking around bewildered. Victoria had dashed across the street to the store to get some additions to supper, but Mums was still sitting in the chair. "Are you feeling better?" she asked, smiling at him.

"Was I feeling bad?"

"You got chilled in the rain," she said.

He nodded vacantly, shivering again as the day came back to him. His mother's terrible rage. The cemetery. "I'm okay," he said without conviction. He started to get up.

"I think you'd better stay in bed," she said. "It's warmer. It wouldn't do to get cold all over again. You might not keep your supper down." He stayed.

Victoria came in a few minutes later with the groceries and an evening paper for Mums from the change. "Hi, Stubs," she said, as if it were perfectly ordinary to see him lying on an old chewed-up mattress on their living-room floor. "Still raining." She took off her jacket and hung it on the line in the bathroom.

Mums still hadn't recovered from her rush to comfort Stubs. Bicks could tell she was in pain by the set of her face.

"Supper's easy tonight," said Victoria. "You read the paper, Mums, and I'll get it on. Then we'll make a rainy-day picnic of it and eat wherever we are, you in your chair, Stubs in his bed, and me where I land." Mums nodded in agreement.

"You can't have a picnic indoors," said Stubs.

"You can when it's raining," she said. "Not much choice." Bicks turned toward the kitchen.

"I'll help," he said.

"Couldn't you be company just once?"

"Don't know. Never been."

"Well, *try* it for a while!" Seeing his face fall, she added, "When I'm ready, you do the serving, okay?"

"Okay."

Stubs ate well but slept badly. He started up screaming five times. The last time Victoria woke him up and told him he'd

36

been snoring, figuring a fresh start on sleep might change the pattern of his dreams. Either it worked or he was finally too exhausted to dream anymore.

She lay awake a long time after that, wondering how long it would take him to really truly get over what his mother had done to him—or if he ever would.

She watched the sunrise, then fell asleep again. A strong feeling that she had something urgent to do woke her. Chalk! The sunrise meant it wasn't raining anymore. She got up and quickly dressed in the bathroom. The chalk was in the kitchen drawer. She was in such a hurry that she decided to let the cockroaches be.

There was a Sunday-morning quiet outside and it was still cool for that time of year. The puddles left from yesterday's rain reflected a cloudless blue sky. There was more than enough dry sidewalk. As she hurried along, she wondered how big the empty circle should be. "Big enough to notice," she decided.

She drew a circle she could put both feet in. She would have liked to have written a message there, too: "Stace! Help!" but didn't dare.

She chalked the circle twice over, then wished on it as hard as she could, shutting her eyes tight and crossing her fingers for luck. And she put a wish on each arrow for good measure. "It's got to work!" she whispered. Little arrows up the rising parts of the front steps and a small circle on the floor in front of their apartment door with a star in the center, figuring that a star had more power than an X.

She let herself in. All was quiet. Stace wouldn't come before Tuesday, she decided. But if she worked, then she couldn't come on Tuesday either. "Won't do any good to stew about it," she said. "It'll work sooner or later, and thinking about it won't hurry it any."

"Huh?" asked Stubs sleepily.

"Oh, nothing. Just talking to myself."

37

"Where you been?" He sat up.

"Out."

"Out where?"

"Making arrows. The sidewalk's dry."

He lay back again. "Won't do no good." He turned his face to the wall.

Bicks figured that he was crying or about to. She went into the kitchen and scalded the cockroaches in the sink, eleven of them, and put the kettle on. She would make instant coffee and hard-boiled eggs. Oatmeal, too, because it was Sunday. The pot roast for dinner was none too big but, with extra potatoes, it would do.

She wondered if Stubs would like to go to church with her. He'd never been, as far as she knew, and he certainly could use the comfort. A loud snuffle from the living room made her decide not to ask him just now. She went, instead, to see if Mums was ready for some coffee.

Her mother was up and dressed and putting on her shoes. "I thought I'd go to church with you," she said.

"Would it be all right?" asked Victoria, thinking of her failing strength.

"It's not far," said Mums, "and I'd like to go." She looked toward the door. "I'm sure Stubs would, too."

"He's in awful misery," Bicks whispered. "I don't know if he can pull himself together."

"Sometimes it helps to have something to pull yourself together for," Mums answered. "I'll talk to him."

She went into the living room, sat in the easy chair, and called Stubs to her side. He came, rubbing his eyes with the heels of his hands, and sat at her feet. Mums laid her head gently on his shoulder and the tears came again. He shook with sobs he couldn't control.

Mums's words seemed, for a while, only to deepen his anguish. It was so awful, the sobbing, that Victoria stood at the sink and

38

cried, too, wiping her eyes now and then with the dishrag. She didn't know that anyone could hurt that much.

All through it, Mums whispered to him, words he couldn't hear, and stroked his hair with her fingers. Little by little he grew quieter, until, except for her murmured words of comfort and an occasional wet sigh from him, all was silent. Victoria knew the worst was over for him. She turned on the oven to make the toast.

Six

All that long week Stubs was quiet, subdued. And Victoria worried about him almost more than she worried about her mother. He didn't refer to his troubles once. He didn't talk about Stace or even mention her name, and when he talked at all, it was about safe things like the weather or stray dogs. Once he noted that the dandelions would be fluff soon, and Victoria translated that into hope.

She waited each night until he was asleep, then quietly stole out and rechalked the arrows. Mums waited up for her to wish her a good night.

"Maybe tomorrow, huh?" asked Victoria.

"Maybe," said Mums.

But tomorrow came and nothing happened. The week dragged by slowly. Victoria was tired from her nocturnal chalkings and was glad when the last bell rang on Friday. She'd fallen asleep twice in spelling, which was her favorite subject, but Miss Seversen, her teacher, pretended not to notice, quietly repeating the words she'd asked Victoria to spell.

Stubs found a dandelion in fluff on the way home. He picked it carefully, then turned his back to Victoria so she wouldn't see how hard he wished, and afterward, he stuffed the stem into his pocket. A little farther along he found one for her.

"No, Stubs, *you* do it," she said.

"Already made my wish," he said, "it's your turn."

Bicks wished double because it was a gift.

That night she used a new piece of chalk. "Maybe tomorrow, huh?"

"Maybe."

Victoria crawled into bed and went instantly to sleep. She dreamed of Stacey. Heard her calling, knew she was searching for Stubs. She wanted to tell her he was here, with them, but something always got in the way and Stacey never heard her. She did keep looking for him, though. She started knocking on doors, asking people had they seen her little brother, Stevie. They shook their heads. Stace turned away. Knocked on another door.

"Not here," one said.

"Ain't seen him."

"No little boys been here."

"Why'd you go and lose him?"

The knocking grew louder. There were whispering voices. Victoria strained to hear what they were saying and woke herself up.

It was well past ten. Stubs's bed was empty and someone was crying. She looked toward the sound. The hall door was wide open. Mums leaned against the frame smiling, though her eyes were shiny with tears.

The chair was in the way. Bicks couldn't see who was there. She got up trailing bedclothes and walked toward the door and back into her dream. Stace knelt in the doorway, her arms around Stubs, and she was crying.

Victoria looked back at her bed to see if she was still there, not fully awake. It took a while for her to realize that the knock-

41

ing she'd heard in her dream was real, that Stacey had followed the chalked arrows and found Stubs; that sometimes wishes come true.

"Is this *now*?" she asked.

"Yes, Bicks, this is now," said Mums. "It's real."

"I went to see her this morning," said Stacey, " 'cause I got a place now and I wanted you to come stay with me."

Stacey sat in the armchair with Stubs on her lap as if she was afraid to let him go. Victoria had gotten dressed and made some coffee. She sat next to her mother on the sofa.

"She didn't know me. Asked who I was, what I wanted. I told her I wanted you, Stevie. She said she didn't know any Stevies, that she never had any kids and had always lived alone. And who was I to come banging on her door asking after someone she'd never heard of?"

Stacey looked down at the Kleenex she'd twisted into a ball. "She looked the same as ever. The place was the same. I saw over her shoulder one cup and one plate on the table. And no sign of Stevie. I asked her what she'd done with you. Where you were. She shut the door in my face.

"I didn't know what to do then. What to think. So I knocked on the caretaker's door and asked him if he'd seen you. And he said, 'Not in a week.' I went out and sat on the steps. If it hadn't been Saturday, I could've gone over to the school and looked for you there. But it was, see. So I'm sitting there staring at the sidewalk and out comes the caretaker's wife and tells me she heard a lot of yelling coming from our apartment about a week ago but didn't look into it 'cause it was none of her business. 'Long as they pay on time,' she goes, 'I don't bother them.' And she hoped that nothing was wrong. I hoped so, too. That was when I saw the chalked circle looking kind of scuffed up and bleary, as if it's been done over and over again. And I wondered if you'd done it . . ."

42

"You remembered!" said Stubs.

"*Sure* I remembered. And if you had, how long you'd been waiting for me to see it. I saw the arrows stretching on down the street. I started to run, calling your name. The caretaker's wife must have thought I'd gone nuts. I saw the little arrows running up the stairs and the star by the door. Then I stopped. I was scared it wasn't you, that I'd be knocking on some stranger's door.

"But I had to find you, you see, and that was the only clue I had. So I knocked and no one answered. Then I knocked a little louder. 'Maybe no one's home,' I thought. I knocked again. And you opened the door," she said, looking at Mums. "You opened the door and smiled and said, 'You must be Stacey,' like you were expecting me.

"I nearly choked I was so happy! And all of a sudden I've got Stevie in my arms and I'm so glad to see him all right, all I could do was cry." She dried her eyes again on the little ball of Kleenex.

"I would have come sooner, only I wanted to get situated. It's not much of a place, Stevie. But it's ours. It'll be lonely for you 'cause I've got me a job, and I'm going to night school to get my diploma. But we'll be together . . ."

"I won't be lonely," said Stubs. "Not when I got you. Lonely's when you got nobody." He leaned back against her, belonging to her. "I'll help around the house, too. Just see if I don't! I'll do the dishes for you and take out the trash and fix your coffee just like Bicks does. I won't need nothing expensive. I got me a new jacket and five dollars. You can have the five dollars . . ."

Stacey laughed and hugged him. "Same old Stevie! Never asking, always giving. We'll start out by having you spend that five dollars on something you don't really need. Something special you want but wouldn't dare say so before."

He looked stunned. "There's nothing I want that I don't have this minute," he said.

43

"Then we'll find something," said Stacey. "Think of it as the only present Mom ever gave you that you didn't have to pay for afterward by feeling guilty 'cause you didn't deserve it."

"I already paid," he said softly, rubbing his neck where the bruises were fading.

Stacey dabbed at her eyes again. "I'm sorry, Stevie. I'm *really* sorry. I should've come sooner. But at first I was so mad, all I could think of was how much I hated her."

"It's okay, Stace. You're here now."

"But after a while the hating wore off. After I'd been away for about a week, I didn't hate her anymore. I felt bad about her, but I didn't hate her. And then I got to thinking what I was going to do next. Running away for spite is one thing, but I didn't want to ruin my life for spite. I thought about you, Stevie, and how things could be better for you if I could find a place. So I started looking for a job, and I found one. Doesn't pay much, but they're willing to train me. And when I get my diploma, they'll see that I get a better job. Never knew that folks were willing to help like that. They were so nice to me. Even offered to help me find somewhere to live that I could afford." She looked up at Victoria's mother. "They think I'm eighteen, you see, and I didn't tell them any different. That way there's no fuss about whether I'm old enough to take care of my brother. And there'll be no trouble for *her*, though I don't know why I should care about that."

"But you do," said Mums. "That's only natural. Is there anything that we can help you with?"

"You've already helped more than I can thank you for, taking Stevie and all. I'm so glad he had friends he could turn to . . ."

There was a loud knock at the door. Stubs jerked as if he had been hit. He watched Victoria go to answer it as if he was afraid that someone had come to take Stacey away from him.

44

"It's all right," said Bicks. "Only a phone call. Shall I see what they want?" Phone calls were very rare, but she wanted to save her mother the agony of the stairs.

Mums nodded.

Victoria shut the door behind her and went down to the pay phone in the front hall, wondering who could be calling them and why. And whether Stubs would ever stop having that kind of reaction to unexpected sounds. And if he would ever stop thinking he was such a nothing-nobody, that whatever he had at any given moment could be taken away from him without upsetting the natural order of things. It was because he had never counted in that order. Bicks understood he couldn't help it. He'd been raised that way. But sometimes she just wanted to take him by the shoulders and shake some sense into him. Maybe with Stace he'd find he was a worthwhile person.

She took up the receiver. "Victoria, dear, is that you?" asked Aunt Millicent. "How is your mother?"

"Mums is fine," said Victoria, crossing her fingers. "Only we've got company just now and they're both just barely done crying so she couldn't come to the phone or they might start right in again and we're almost out of Kleenex."

"You're what?"

"Almost out of Kleenex. My friends Stubs, you see—his mom threw him out and he's been staying with us until we could find his sister. She just got here and they've been crying because they're so glad to be together, and we're almost out of Kleenex. So Mums couldn't leave them or they'd start right in again. See?"

"I'm not sure I do," said Aunt Millicent. "But I did want to talk to your mother. I haven't had one word from her in months and it's worrying me."

"I guess she just forgot to write," said Victoria.

"Is she working?"

45

"Not right now. She's had a cold, you see, and she's got to be careful when she catches a cold . . ."

"A bad one?"

"Not so bad. It's about gone."

"I hope so," said Aunt Millicent. "I *do* worry about her. When are you coming down here?"

"Oh. Well. We, um. We haven't made any plans yet. I still have school . . ."

"When is school out?"

"Not for a whole week."

"What day?"

Victoria told her.

"Then the very next day you pack up and come on down. Plan on staying the whole summer at the least. That'll give me plenty of time to persuade your mother to make it permanent. Do you need bus fare or anything?"

"We've got bus fare," said Victoria.

"Then I'll be expecting you soon. Give my love to your mother."

"I will," said Victoria. "Aunt Millicent . . ." she began. She stopped. What she wanted to say was "Mums is sick. She's dying, Aunt Millicent. Dying soon, and I'm so scared!"

She didn't say it. ". . . thanks for calling."

"Quite all right, dear. It's been nice to talk to you, and it'll be even nicer when we're all together again. Why Alison insists on living way up there, I'll never understand. Mind you, the very next day after school's out."

"I'll tell Mums what you said."

Victoria stood by the phone for several minutes after she'd hung up, wishing she'd told Aunt Millicent the truth, but feeling that, if she had, it would have been like a betrayal. The least trouble for the fewest people, that's what Mums said. She would die here and be buried here. She did not want to burden Aunt Millicent with her illness and death. If it seemed a little

46

like getting even, well, it couldn't be mended now. Mums was too sick to travel. No amount of rest seemed to help her anymore, and sometimes she woke in the night with pain. There was nothing Victoria could do for her.

Slowly, she started up the stairs.

Seven

Stubs bundled up his belongings, and Stacey folded the blanket and sheet so that they could take the mattress back down to the cellar. Mums looked spent. Victoria got her back to bed. And then there were goodbyes.

"Listen, Stubs," said Victoria, "why don't you take this with you?" She put the blanket and sheet on top of his bundle. "We won't be needing it anymore."

"But that's a perfectly good blanket!" Stubs objected.

"All the more reason it should have some use."

"I can't take your spare blanket."

"We're not going to need it ever again," said Victoria.

Stubs got the point. "So soon?"

She nodded. "It's all right, Stubs. I'm used to the idea. And, anyway, I can't take *everything* with me."

Stacey looked puzzled.

"Stubs'll tell you later," said Victoria. She sort of smiled. "I'm glad you remembered the arrows. Maybe I can come and see you sometime. When you get settled in and all . . ."

"We'll have you over to a party dinner come next payday," said Stacey.

48

"I'd like that," said Victoria. She went down to the street with them and watched while they walked away. She could tell by the way Stubs walked that he was really running off at the mouth. Making up, in a rush, for all that long, silent week of waiting. He tripped over a crack in the sidewalk and Stacey put out her hand to steady him. A steadying hand; he needed it more than most.

Suddenly Victoria felt very alone and very hungry. In all the excitement of Stacey's appearing at their place to claim her brother, no one had had anything to eat. It was already past lunchtime. She hurried in.

Mums was asleep. Bicks went about on tiptoe, clearing away the coffee cups, neatening up the room. Mrs. Jardine knocked on the door. She wanted to know if the phone call was bad news. The phone was just outside her door so she felt a proprietary interest in it. Hearing only half a conversation was highly unsatisfactory.

Bicks stepped out into the hall to talk to her. "Mums is sleeping," she explained.

"Hear she has a cold," said Mrs. Jardine. "Come to think of it, I haven't seen her about much lately. Must be a nasty one, that cold."

"She gets them now and then," said Victoria. She didn't exactly dislike Mrs. Jardine, but she wasn't comfortable with her either. She didn't volunteer anything more.

"A nasty one," Mrs. Jardine repeated. "Had one myself this past winter. Thought I'd never get over it. Six times I went to see the doc. Cost enough. I spent a bundle on pills that didn't do a damn bit of good. What's your ma taking for hers?"

"For her cold? Oh, nothing. She's just waiting it out."

"Just waiting it out, huh? Don't know as I'd do that, myself. Never can tell with a cold. Might be something else, you know."

"It's just a cold."

49

"So you say." Mrs. Jardine looked her up and down in a way that clearly showed she doubted Victoria's word. "So you say." She dismissed that tack and went straight to her main point. As a rule she was so skillful at prying that she never had to use the direct approach, but Victoria was not cooperating.

"That phone call wasn't bad news, I hope."

"No."

"Your aunt okay?"

"She's fine."

"Just calling to say hello, huh?"

"She wants us to come visit her." Victoria wished she hadn't volunteered so much all at once.

"Whereabouts does she live?"

"Iowa."

"Iowa. Been to Iowa once myself."

"So have I."

"Iowa. You going?"

"We haven't talked about it yet."

"Not decided, huh? Don't like your aunt, I'll bet."

"I'll bet I do!" There now, Mrs. Jardine had her riled, which was one of her techniques.

"Your mom don't like her."

Bicks struggled against making a smart remark. It didn't do to be rude, even though all this was none of her business. She realized that if Stacey or Stubs had asked her who was on the phone she'd have told them the whole conversation without even batting an eye. It was just that Mrs. Jardine got her back up. Interested was one thing, nosiness another. And eavesdropping, well, there was no excuse for that!

"Aunt Millicent is one of Mums's favorite people."

"Millicent, huh? I knew a Millicent once."

Victoria fought the impulse to say, "Good for you," saying instead, "Her name is Purvis. Millicent Purvis."

50

"Your Aunt Millicent. She must have a pretty big place asking two to come visit her. She rich?"

"Not really."

Mrs. Jardine gave up. She couldn't buck Victoria's resistance. "Well, when you go visit that aunt of yours, rich or not, you send me a card, huh? I don't get much mail."

"I'll do that," said Victoria.

A parting shot to catch her off base. "When are you going?"

"Don't know."

"Just a bit of advice," said Mrs. Jardine, as she started down the stairs. "When you got a rich relation and they phone you up to come visit, you jump! You get yourself down there as fast as you can! Just a bit of advice from an old woman. Take it or leave it."

"Thanks," said Victoria. It would've been so easy to push that woman down the stairs. With admirable restraint, Bicks stood there smiling as Mrs. Jardine lumbered slowly down.

"Just a bit of advice, mind."

"Yes," said Victoria, letting her go with her erroneous conclusion: that Aunt Millicent was rich. Owning a house didn't make you rich and Aunt Millicent worked just like anyone else. She went in and quietly shut the door behind her, though the urge to slam it was almost more than she could master. "Busybody!" she exclaimed.

Bicks made herself a cheese sandwich, then turned on the oven to toast it. The trouble with Mrs. Jardine was that she didn't have enough to do. Weekdays she got all dressed up and went downtown to where she banked and watched soap operas in the social room. The rest of the time she spent keeping track of her neighbors and speculating on their comings and goings. She never invited anyone in, and she never, never went out at night, for fear of being robbed and murdered. Even in broad daylight she carried her purse as if it were packed with diamonds,

51

in both hands, tight against her chest. She was really pretty pathetic, Victoria decided, though that didn't justify her eavesdropping.

The sandwich was good, but it set her to worrying about grocery money. They'd spent much more than they usually did in the past week, feeding three instead of two. She wondered how she could stretch what was left to the end of the month. And then she wondered if she'd have to. She dismissed *that* thought right away.

"She's just tired," she said to herself, "because of the strain of having company. That's it. A day or two of quiet will fix her up." Not that Stubs had been all that noisy, at least not after the first day. It was wearing, though, to have an extra worry. And what would they have done with Stubs if Stacey hadn't come for him?

They hadn't talked about that. They couldn't have found the opportunity, anyway, with just three little rooms and nowhere to go for a quiet talk. But Victoria had already decided that if Stace didn't show before . . . well . . . before she had to go away, she would find a way to take Stubs with her, even if they had to walk. And Stubs would've had to go because he didn't have any place else.

She decided to go out and wash the arrows off the steps. Let the rain and passing feet do for the others. They'd done their job and it was a great relief.

She got a damp rag and, skipping over the star by the door, began to work her way down the stairs. Quietly, so as not to interest Mrs. Jardine.

The phone rang as she got to the front hall. She hurried past it and ducked out the door. It kept ringing. Ten, eleven, twelve, then stopped. Mrs. Jardine was out and no one else bothered.

Bicks started down the front steps. Three to go. She wanted to get done before Mrs. Jardine got back with her questions. A

52

shadow fell across her and the blackened stairs. She looked up, thinking it was Mrs. Jardine.

Beulah Martin, Stubs's mom, stood over her. Victoria stared at her for a moment, stunned. There was no recognition in her face. Nothing that indicated she knew Victoria. Bicks tried to shrink away, but Mrs. Martin moved quickly to cut off her retreat.

She looked old and spent. But the hand that clutched Bicks's shoulder was strong. Too strong.

"You've seen it," she said. "Where is it?" The tone low, intense.

Bicks tried to pull away. The grip tightened. She tried to think how to get free and found herself staring at the woman's other hand. The fingernails were cracked and broken, some so close to the quick that they'd bled. A distraction, she needed some kind of distraction. "How did you hurt your hand?" she asked.

"My hand?" Anger. "There's nothing wrong with my hand!"

"It's been bleeding," said Bicks. "You ought to take care of it."

"It's not my blood," she said, "it belongs to someone else."

Bicks shuddered. It very well could have been Stubs's blood. She understood his terror better now. It was a miracle he had escaped at all. She was so strong and her eyes were very strange. The dark part way too big. Like night eyes even though the sun was bright. She seemed to be looking through Victoria to something else. "I want it," she said. "Where is it?"

"I don't know," said Bicks, twisting under the clutching hand. She was released unexpectedly and nearly tumbled down the stairs. She saw the change come over Mrs. Martin, the change that Stubs had described only too well, and fled up the front stairs, slamming the street door behind her. She leaned against

53

that door, breathless with the awfulness of it. No wonder Stubs had cried out in his sleep!

After a minute, she opened the door a crack and peeped out. The street was busy at that hour. Mrs. Martin was angrily accosting passers-by. Pulling at their arms, demanding to know what they'd done with it, where was it, why'd you take it?

Bicks opened the door a little wider, but she didn't dare step out. Mrs. Jardine was out there carrying a loaf of bread. Mrs. Martin spun her around and nearly knocked her down. She dropped the bread. A man picked it up and handed it back to her. Mrs. Martin turned on him and he gave her rage for rage. "Get off the street, you loony!" he shouted. "Get out of here!"

She reacted as if she had been slapped across the face. Her head actually snapped back and she raised her arms as if to ward off another blow. When it didn't come, she looked around as if she was dazed. The man had taken his anger down the street and Mrs. Jardine was hurrying away. Mrs. Martin stumbled a few steps after her, but a tremor stopped her. There was horror in the change. Horror of herself and what she might have done. She got her bearings and started up the street. In haste to escape, not looking where she was going, she ran into Mrs. Jardine, making her drop her bread again.

"Watch where you're going, you old bag!" she said.

"Well!" Mrs. Jardine managed indignantly. "Well! I never!"

Victoria ran down the steps and picked up the bread.

"Did you see that?" Mrs. Jardine asked. "Crazy as they come! What're things getting to when they let people like that wander around loose? Did you see that?"

"What did she want?" asked Bicks, handing her the loaf of bread.

"Nothing as far as I could tell. Except to bother a poor old lady. 'Where is it?' she said. That's all. Did you ever see the like?"

54

"No, guess I haven't."

"She ought to be locked up, that's what! And if I ever see her again, I'm going to call the police. I am."

"Oh, don't do *that!*" said Victoria quickly.

"Why not? It's not safe to walk the streets with her kind knocking you down at every turn!"

"She . . . well . . . she used to be the mother of a friend of mine."

Mrs. Jardine looked at Bicks severely over the rims of her glasses. "What do you mean, 'used to be'?" she asked.

"Oh, nothing. She was his mother and now she isn't."

"Died, huh?"

Bicks didn't answer one way or the other.

"Probably crazy with grief, huh?"

"Could be," said Victoria. "Anyway, she can't help the way she is."

"Yes," said Mrs. Jardine. "I can see that. I've heard it happens. Not that I ever had a kid myself. But grieving takes you in peculiar ways." She stopped at her door and dug in her purse for her keys. "Suppose I won't call the police on her. What would they know about grief, huh? Now, when my Herman passed on . . ." She dropped her bread again. Victoria picked it up. "Thanks, dear. Now, when my Herman passed on, I couldn't eat sardines in mustard for five years, he had liked them so much. Every time I'd try to eat them, I'd think of him and go on a crying jag. Just crazy with mourning. It takes you in peculiar ways. I still get a little sentimental over sardines. He had the gout, you know. Couldn't move about much when it was on him. And then his heart went bad. Died right here in the hall. Flopped right over and died, and there wasn't anything they could do for him."

She finally got her door open. "It takes some getting over when you lose someone you're fond of . . ." Her voice trailed

55

off and she shut the door in Victoria's face as if she weren't even there.

Bicks didn't mind. It was as good a way as any to end the conversation. Bolting off, mid-sentence, would've been impolite. She retrieved her damp rag and gave the last three arrows a swipe. "You can bet," she said to herself, "I'd never cry over sardines and mustard! You just bet I wouldn't!"

Eight

Mums was in pain all that weekend. Aspirin helped for a little while, but the pain, after the short relief, always seemed heavier afterward. Not that she complained, she never did that. But the pain was visible as it played over her thin, pinched face like moving lights over dark water. And when Victoria was near her, she could feel it quivering and radiating like a live thing.

They talked for a while, with many long pauses, of Aunt Millicent's telephone call. Only one of them would answer her invitation. They did not speak of that. "I'll try to write to her this week," said Mums, shutting her eyes against the pain.

Victoria, watching her, wondered if she would be able to. "I'll get you a stamp," she said. But she didn't jump up then and there to go out to get one. It could wait until there was something to put it on, if there ever was.

Bicks had just begun to start supper on Sunday evening when she heard a long-drawn-out sigh. She hurried into the room where Mums sat propped up in the easy chair. "Mums?"

"It's all right, Bicks." Mums smiled at her. The pain was gone. "It's all right. I think I'd like to sleep for a while now."

Mums hadn't slept much during those two days and there

57

were dark hollows under her eyes. She dozed off immediately. Victoria watched her for a few minutes, then tiptoed back to the kitchen and sat on the floor hugging her knees. That long sigh had scared her. Tears of relief rolled down her cheeks, but she made no sound except, now and then, a shaky intake of breath.

She would have to face it soon. Her mother's death. She knew there couldn't be much time left. Say goodbye forever. Say I love you. Say I want you near me. Say goodbye.

It had been a cold. Everybody got colds. Every day of the year someone got over a cold. But not Mums. One cold she got when she was a kid, doctors said years afterward, was rheumatic fever. It was when Victoria was born that they diagnosed it, she'd been so weak afterward. There was damage to her heart. With care she could lead a normal life, but no more children. They had all lived with Aunt Millicent for a long time while Mums got well.

And when she was well, really well, they'd moved to Minneapolis. Victoria's father had a good job and they lived in a little rented house not far from the river. Then came Vietnam and a long, anxious time. He came home without a scratch, although he'd changed. He didn't smile as often anymore, and his face, in repose, looked old and sad. And then he was gone. A fork lift failed and he was crushed under its load. He was gone.

"Say goodbye, Victoria." Row after row of white stones. "Say goodbye."

After that Mums got a job. With care, a normal life. But worry and sorrow took its toll and her health begin to fail in little bits and pieces. She would walk more slowly and sometimes stop to admire a view that wasn't particularly worthy of notice. Victoria caught on and began to invent pauses when she could tell Mums was out of breath, little games to mask her growing concern.

58

That's when she began to count up the piper's payment and collect dead cockroaches for revenge. To get even with the world because her mother had to die.

When it was all over she was going to send that box of cockroaches to someone. That was the part she hadn't sorted out. Who would get the awful gift? Who was to blame? Whose fault was it that she was in this wretched place, sitting on the cracked linoleum, waiting for her mother to die?

No one. No one at all. It's just the way things are. They happen that way. But *why?* Victoria wanted to shout it out. "Why?" And she wanted an answer beyond because. But there was no answer. And there were no miracles left.

Say goodbye forever.

It wasn't fair! It just wasn't fair! But was anything? What *was* fair? Was good luck fair? If you had good luck and someone else didn't, was that fair? And Stubs. Was it fair what happened to him? Hated for ten years, then thrown out on the street, lucky to be alive? What was the answer? Bicks shook her head. It was too hard to understand. She didn't know and she wondered if anyone did.

Mums stirred in her sleep. Victoria got up and went to her. To see that she was all right. To adjust the blanket. The evenings were cool though it was June. It was nearly dark, but she didn't turn on the light. She sat down on the sofa to wait out her mother's sleep.

Why was no good. Because after why came why not. If was too wishful. A whole basketful of ifs couldn't change things. Because was so lame it wasn't worth its seven letters.

Change. Change, that was it. There were things you could change. There were things that you couldn't. And, somehow, you had to manage in between. Stacey had run away because she couldn't change the situation at home. It was out of her control. But she could do something about her own life, and

59

Stubs's. Change the things you *can* handle and live with the rest, since you've got no choice in the matter.

The hard part was living with the rest. She sighed. Sometimes you were strong and sometimes you were fragile. When you were strong you could think about the hard part, but when you felt fragile, you'd better think about the weather and stray dogs.

"Victoria?"

A little louder. "Bicks, are you there?"

Victoria sat up suddenly. She hadn't meant to fall asleep. "Yes, Mums, right here. I'll turn on the light."

She jumped up and flipped the light switch, blinked at the clock. Nearly ten and no supper. She hurried to the stove and bustled around getting their meal started.

The sleep had helped. Mums looked a little better. The pain was gone. Victoria felt a flicker of hope rising, maybe not so soon.

Mums ate well, which pleased Victoria. She chattered through the meal, telling Mums of Mrs. Jardine and how she couldn't eat sardines in mustard for five years after her mister died.

"I couldn't eat sardines in mustard ever!" said Victoria. "Not in a hundred, thousand, million years, I couldn't."

Mums was curious about that story because Mrs. Jardine almost never talked about herself.

"I think she was a little flustered after dropping her loaf of bread so many times. It got all squashed. Stubs's Mom . . ." Bicks stopped.

"What about her?"

Victoria told Mums what she had seen. "What do you think she was looking for, anyway?"

"Stubs. Only maybe she doesn't realize it."

"I'd better *tell* him!"

60

"I don't know. Did she recognize you?"

"Me? She didn't know me at all! It was as if a part of her was missing." Bicks paused for a minute, thinking. "I wonder," she went on, "what she would've done if I'd told her Stubs had been here. Nothing, I suppose. She didn't know Stace at all, and she said she'd never heard of any Stevies. What's wrong with her, anyway?"

"I don't know," said Mums. "I just don't know."

"You know what I think?" asked Victoria. "I think she's crazy. Throwing out a perfectly good kid like Stubs and saying afterward that she'd never heard of anyone of that name. It's as if he didn't exist at all, as if she'd never known him. Of course, she never thought much of him anyway, so I guess forgetting all about him isn't such a surprise, huh?"

"Perhaps not," said Mums. After a minute, she added, "I don't think it would help Stubs if you told him about what you saw today. But you might tell Stacey if you see her and can talk to her privately."

"Okay, Mums," said Victoria. "I'd just as soon not tell him, anyway. It would only worry him." She rose to clear away the dishes. "You know, we forgot all about asking Stace for their address." She carried the plates out to the sink and came back for the rest of the things.

"When you see him at school tomorrow," said Mums, "you can ask him where they live."

While Victoria washed the dishes, Mums took a long, hot bath, and after Bicks was in bed, she came to her and sat on the edge of her bed. She wished her a good night as she used to do when Victoria was very little and scared of the dark, talking to her until the night fears went away and she fell asleep.

It didn't take long. Victoria was very tired. After a few minutes, Mums got up and went out to the kitchen. There was a candle on the shelf. She lit it, stuck it to a saucer, and, shielding

61

it with her hand, returned to Victoria's bedside and looked down on her as she lay sleeping.

She stood there for a long time, until the candle burned low, sputtered, and went out. "Good night, Victoria," she whispered. "I love you."

Nine

The morning began in a dead heat with Victoria racing neck and neck against the clock. She'd forgotten to set it and it was paying her back by running fast; at least, that's how it seemed. She had time for only the barest of necessities: getting dressed; a slight comb and a wash; peanut butter on bread rolled up and jammed into her pocket; and a hurried cup of coffee for Mums, sloshed over the saucer. Bicks saw that Mums was sleeping and set the coffee down on the nightstand and left for school. No pain now, Mums smiled in her sleep.

Victoria ran down the street, stopping now and then to catch her breath and take a bite of the bread. Peanut butter and hurry didn't go well together, but it was better than going hungry until lunchtime. Second lunch, at that. Stubs had first lunch so she would have to wait to see him after school.

The warning bell rang just as she reached the playground. She tripped and fell in her rush, and dropped the last bit of bread in the dirt.

"Lie there, then!" she exclaimed, picking herself up. She slipped into her seat just as the tardy bell rang.

Because it was the last Monday of the school year, it was an easy day. Miss Seversen didn't even try to fight the year-end

63

fidgets. Summer was beckoning outside the open windows and no one could compete with that. Miss Seversen did make a slight show of trying, but read them stories without discussion after her first futile attempt. No one seemed able to follow the line of a story, at least not to the point of answering a question about it. So she read on, enjoying the story herself, hoping, maybe, that some of it would sink in.

Victoria slipped into daydreams and what-ifs against the rhythm of the quiet voice rising and falling. It was a shimmery day, full of gold, that made promises it couldn't keep.

The what-ifs fueled the daydreams and Bicks saw herself and Mums walking up a low hill in the hot August sun, gathering goldenrod, the long, dry grass stalks rustling against their legs as they walked. Mums laughed to see a striped gopher that froze in their path, eyeing them, only to scurry away without a sound, moving so fast it seemed that all the spots and stripes ran together. Then she laughed again for sheer joy. It was so good to be well again. So good to walk freely, without pain. To breathe the clean-scented air. To watch the sun go down in a pool of gold.

The bell rang for second lunch and the howling stampede jolted Bicks. She looked around, startled. Then at the floor, as if to see where she'd dropped her goldenrod. Her daydream had seemed so real.

But she was hungry. That was real, too. She got up and followed her classmates to the lunchroom.

Pizza and a sweet roll, corn and chocolate milk, ice cream on a stick. The windows vibrated with shouts of delight. The monitors, usually so particular about quiet in the lunchroom, played deaf and dumb, and lunch progressed in a roar.

It was, for that time of year, a well-planned meal. The food served was universally popular and none of it ended up on the walls, though many ice-cream sticks were smuggled out to become missiles during the long, very likely dull afternoon.

64

Bicks traded her sweet roll and her ice-cream stick for someone's slice of pizza and made a good lunch of the bargain. Sweet rolls were any-day things, but she never got pizza except at school. "Just make sure you don't aim that stick at me!" she said.

"Won't," said the boy, "see?" He opened his fist and revealed a handful of cooked corn.

"Don't aim *that* at me, either," she said.

"You wouldn't *tell?*" he asked.

"Don't count on it."

"All right," he agreed. "But others saved their corn besides me, so if you get hit, don't look my way."

It was going to be a messy afternoon, Bicks thought. Too bad they couldn't have served up a one-piece vegetable, like a giant green bean, one to a customer. At any rate, corn was neater than peas, having more character when cooked. Peas went splat.

Miss Seversen managed to ignore all except the worst of it. But no one was sent up to the office. She merely confiscated the corn and sticks.

Miss Seversen was okay. She was really strict most of the time, but she knew she could relax the rules now and then without losing control. Bicks liked her better than any teacher she'd ever had before.

She would've gone straight home after school to escape the corn barrage, but she had to wait around in hopes of catching Stubs. She'd promised Mums that she would get his address.

It seemed like an endless wait. And when he finally came out, hard on the heels of his liberated class, he looked like a different kid. Victoria would have passed by him on the street had he not run up to her and said, "Hullo, Bicks." True, he was all over the same person. But there was something else. Something shining out of him that she'd never seen before. It was staggering what a little care could do for a ratty-looking kid like Stubs!

"How're things going?" she asked.

65

"Just swell!" He beamed. You know what we're doing Sunday? We're going to take the bus clear across town and go to Como Zoo! I've never been to the zoo. Ever! You been?"

"Not to remember." Victoria felt a tiny tug of envy. "That's great, Stubs!" she said. "That's really great!"

"Maybe you'd like to come too, huh?"

"Gee . . ." Bicks was awfully tempted. "I guess I'd better not. Mums . . ." she said.

"Oh. Yeah. Sure. Listen, I have to hurry. Got a lot of things to do before Stace gets home. I'm going to clean up the kitchen and fix her supper. Like you do. Only maybe not so good. Takes a while to get the hang of it." He started to hurry away.

"Hey, Stubs!" Bicks called. "Wait! What's your address?"

"Address?"

"You know. Where you live."

"You mean like street and all that?"

"Yes."

Stubs looked puzzled. He scratched his head, and stood on one foot and then the other. "Gee, Bicks," he said, "I don't know."

"Don't know! Why, everyone knows where they live!"

"For sure I know *that!*" he said. "I only don't know what it's called, that's all. I know how to *get* there. Why don't you come on home with me and see it?"

"I'd like to," said Bicks hesitating, "but best not. I left in such a rush this morning that I didn't fix Mums her breakfast. Tell you what. Why don't you write it down and give it to me tomorrow?"

"Sure thing," said Stubs. "See ya!" He trotted off, Bicks watching. A way up the street he stopped and picked up a stick, then went on, half jogging, now and then making a feint to the side to whack a parking meter or a signpost with the stick, leaping aside as if the post struck back, sometimes making a complete turnabout in the process, like a frisky colt. He skipped up to a

66

stop sign, fenced it into submission, and went on, one foot in the gutter, the other on the curb, until he found a tin can he took for a hockey puck and so worked his way around a corner and disappeared from view.

Bicks sighed and turned toward home, her steps slow and heavy. It seemed as if all the light had gone out of the day, though the sun was still shining brightly. Maybe, she thought, it was just the contrast between Stubs's mood and hers. Maybe . . .

"Penny for your thoughts, Victoria."

She looked up. Miss Seversen had come up beside her on her way to the bus stop.

"They're not worth a penny," said Victoria.

"Why not?"

"Oh, I don't know. Wasn't thinking much, that's all."

"You looked as if you had the weight of the world on your shoulders," said Miss Seversen.

Victoria shook her head. They walked on in silence. They had nearly reached the bus stop when Miss Seversen asked, "Is anything wrong, Victoria? Anything you'd like to talk about?"

"No. Nothing's wrong," said Bicks, walking a little faster.

"Are you sure? It seems to me that you're worrying about something. Couldn't you tell me about it?"

"There isn't anything to tell," said Bicks, making herself smile. "Everything's fine. Just fine."

Miss Seversen didn't buy Bicks's answer, but her bus was coming and the Number 2 didn't run very often. "Maybe we can talk tomorrow," she said as she got on the bus. Victoria stood for a minute watching it get smaller as it traveled down the street. "Maybe we can talk tomorrow." She shook her head and walked on.

"I'll tell her my kitten died," she said to herself. "If it comes to talking about anything." It wouldn't be a lie. She had had a kitten and the kitten had died. More than a year ago. "I'll tell her about that."

67

She decided she would have to look more cheerful the next day. Maybe Miss Seversen would notice and put off their talk. Bicks knew she wasn't proof against too many questions, and the bus hadn't come a second too soon. One more gentle query from Miss Seversen and she would've spilled her worries all over the street. Maybe Miss Seversen would forget all about it.

When Bicks let herself in, Mums didn't call to her, so she assumed she was sleeping. She got some change from the jar in the kitchen and ran down to the corner to get an afternoon paper. Mums enjoyed the paper. She would also enjoy hearing about Stubs, how he didn't know his address but just how to get there.

Victoria tossed the paper onto the table and banged the door shut behind her. "Hi, Mums!" she called out. "I'm home!"

There was no answer.

"Mums?" Victoria felt icy needles through her heart. "Mums?" No answer.

She hurried into the bedroom. The sun slanted through the window, throwing a block of light across the bed. Mums lay there, apparently sleeping, a smile on her face. The cup of coffee on the nightstand hadn't been touched. The sloshes were dry in the saucer.

Bicks shook her gently. "Mums? Wake up, Mums!" she pleaded. "Please wake up!"

Her hands were cold. Victoria got a blanket and spread it over her. She was cold. Terribly cold. That was it! She was too cold to wake up. Yes, that was it.

"I'll make you some hot coffee," said Victoria. She took the cup and saucer out to the kitchen and rinsed them out.

"She's just cold," said Victoria. "Some hot coffee . . ."

She set the cup down and, drying her hands on her jeans, went back to the bedroom. The shaft of sunlight dwindled and disappeared. Mums lay as before. There was no change, in spite of the blanket. Victoria stood beside the bed, watching her, waiting for a sign.

68

But there was no change. Bit by bit the awareness stole over her that she was alone. All alone. The figure on the bed did not move. There was no rising and falling of the blanket to indicate the intake of breath. There was no one there. Mums was gone. Her body was empty. "When I don't answer you . . ."

And still Victoria stood there. Waiting. Dusk came, the traffic in the street diminished, though she didn't notice it. She waited for one thing only. She waited to hear Mums call her name. "Is that you, Victoria?" She waited for her to start breathing again.

Night fell without stars. Victoria stood by the bed, waiting.

It couldn't be! It couldn't! There had been no goodbyes. She groped for the cold hand in the dark. No goodbyes.

Say goodbye, Victoria.

"I can't, Mums, I can't!"

Say goodbye forever.

"Not yet, Mums. Please. Not yet."

Say goodbye.

Ten

Victoria woke at dawn as the gray light widened in the room. She was curled up on a corner of the sofa, fully dressed. She didn't know how she'd gotten there. She couldn't remember leaving the bedroom.

She lay there, watching the light grow, not wanting to move. Not wanting to get up and do what she had to do next. Not willing to face the brightness of the day. Why couldn't the night have been longer? She wasn't ready for the day. She wasn't ready to keep the promise she'd made to Mums.

She shut her eyes and tried to go back to sleep. As long as she slept, she wouldn't have to do anything. But sleep would not come.

She lay instead, listening to the street noises outside, wishing for yesterday. No, the day before yesterday. Any time in the past, but not today. She didn't want today. She also knew she couldn't wish hard enough for that. Mums was dead and there were no miracles.

Victoria got up and went to the bathroom. She washed her face. In the cracked mirror she looked just the same as she had yesterday, except that today she was not in a hurry. She was shocked that it didn't show; Mums was dead and it didn't show in her face. It didn't seem right.

She went into the kitchen and automatically scalded the cockroaches that were in the sink, laying them up on the shelf to dry.

There were Mums's cup and saucer from the day before. Bicks put them back in the cupboard. They hadn't really been used. There was the knife with the peanut butter dried and cracked on it. She stared at it, wondering how she could've forgotten to rinse that off. She'd been in such a hurry.

If she hadn't been in such a hurry . . .

If she'd taken time to see that Mums was all right . . .

If she'd done that . . .

Maybe . . .

She saw herself, yesterday morning, rushing into the bedroom with a comb stuck in her hair. Saw the coffee sloshed into the saucer. Saw Mums lying there, a smile on her face as if her dreams gave her joy.

"No," said Victoria.

Then again, "No."

She looked toward the bedroom, walked slowly to the door, and entered the room. She looked down at her mother, at her smile. It was the same.

Victoria went into the living room and sat on the lopsided easy chair. The smile was the same. It was a wisp of comfort that Mums hadn't died all alone. She'd died in her sleep. Victoria was there when she died. She hadn't been alone.

And now? What was she to do now? The money was under the pillow—the bus fare to Dubuque.

Wasn't there more to it?

All the arrangements had been made. Everything was taken care of. The money order. The bus fare. If she could keep back the tears for a little while, then everything would be all right.

71

No, not all right, but it had to be endured. There was nothing else she *could* do.

And Victoria saw it now, the flaw in the arrangements. She was the only one who knew that her mother was dead. If she left Mums lying there and went to Aunt Millicent's, then no one would ever know she was dead and gone. At least not for a long while. And how would anyone else know she'd already planned her own burial? It would happen all wrong!

She would have to do something about that. What, she didn't know. She would have to figure it out. Whatever it was, whatever had to be done to make things right, she would have to see it through. But she couldn't think just sitting there. She had to *do* something.

Victoria stood up and looked around. She would clean house and she would pack. The tidying up would make it easier to pack.

Victoria set to work. It didn't take very long. The apartment was neither very big nor very dirty.

She began to sort. One always sorts when things come to an end. She got out the big plastic shopping bag. A few clothes and treasures would go in that. What she couldn't carry herself she would put in a box addressed to Aunt Millicent and hope that someone would send it. She needed a box.

Bicks took her key and went out, locking the door behind her. She listened, for a moment, in the hall. Sure that no one was about, she went quietly down the stairs and out the front door. The store across the street would have boxes.

The phone rang in the hall. Mrs. Jardine answered it. "Who?" she asked. She was annoyed that the phone had rung just then. She was about to leave the house for her daily outing.

"Purvis? Not in school, huh? Well, I'll check for you, but they aren't likely to answer."

Mrs. Jardine set the phone down and hollered up the stairs

72

for Purvis. When there was no response, she climbed the stairs and knocked loudly on the door. No one answered. She tried the knob and found it locked. She shrugged and went back to the phone.

"No one's home," she said. "Heard they were going down to Iowa to visit some rich relation. Des Moines. Some place like that." She hung up the phone and went back into her apartment to gather up her purse and her umbrella. Not that it looked like rain, but you never could tell. She was out the door and down the steps before the phone could catch her again.

There was a bus coming. She scurried to the corner, pulling on her gloves as she went. She did not see Victoria cross the street, mid-block, carrying a couple of boxes. And, once on the bus, she had to fumble in her purse for her senior citizen's pass. Victoria climbed the steps with her boxes, unnoticed. But she had seen Mrs. Jardine and knew that, when she had screwed up her courage to use the phone, she would be able to make her call in privacy.

Bicks let herself in and set the boxes down by the door. The other she would label for the Goodwill.

She felt a sudden dizziness and the room went all spotty for a minute. Food. She hadn't had anything to eat since yesterday's lunch. She went into the kitchen and fixed herself some scrambled eggs on bread, a glass of milk, and some orange juice. She felt sick, but only for a moment.

The food helped. She felt stronger and the tears were further away. She opened the sofa bed and took out her things. The box of cockroaches. She didn't feel like revenge. Stubs had liked them so she decided to leave them for him, to remember her by. She tied a string around the shoebox and wrote his name on it. Maybe, somehow, he would get it. She didn't know where he lived.

There was a little photo album. Victoria wrapped it in her

73

windbreaker and put it in the shopping bag. That was one thing she *must* have. There were few other treasures as important to her.

Her father's watch. Mums kept it in the drawer of her nightstand, always wound. It had run down. Bicks wound it and let it run from where it had stopped. She didn't know what time it was. It didn't much matter. She had no schedule to keep. She buckled it on to a belt loop of her jeans. It was too big for her to wear.

The alarm clock, which had stopped during the night, went into the box for the Goodwill. It was a good clock and someone would find use for it. Things that were tattered or cracked she left where they were, for someone else to discard.

How long she spent in her sorting, she didn't know. But, little by little, she felt her will harden, like ice forming over a pool. When it was strong enough to walk on, she would be able to call the funeral home.

Victoria finished her work. She sat down on one of the hard chairs and looked around the room. She wouldn't miss it. There was nothing attractive about it, and the only reason for staying there was gone. There was no shred of comfort left in the shabby room. Only two more things to do, and then the phone call.

She went into the bedroom. It was the time of day when the sunlight found its way in, but there was no sun. From a bright beginning the day had gone all soft and gray. Victoria took the envelope out from under her mother's pillow. In it she found the check, the bus fare, and a twice-folded piece of paper. Her name was on it.

A crack in the ice. Bicks stuffed the paper with her name on it into her pocket. She could not look at it now. She had nothing to put the bus fare in except Mums's purse. But she would look funny carrying that. She put the money in it and put it in the shopping bag.

74

Bicks looked at the check, then returned it to the envelope, sealed it, and pinned it to her undershirt. It could have gone into the purse, but Mums had told her to pin it to her undershirt.

One more thing to do. Then she would make the phone call.

Victoria opened the cabinet that they used for a closet and took out Mums's good dress. The one with the skinny blue stripes. She folded it carefully and laid it at the foot of the bed along with the things Mums would have worn with it. She kissed the cold forehead. Still, she could not say goodbye, not yet.

She wondered if she had taken too much time in her sorting, if Mrs. Jardine was back from downtown. Because she couldn't face her questions, she decided to use the phone booth across the street.

They were very nice at the funeral home. They understood grief and handled her caringly, accepting the fiction of friend of the family. She'd used her teacher's name, knowing that her own would not do. Yes, the arrangements had been completed some months ago. Purvis. No visitation. Simple graveside services. It was all taken care of. If she would be so kind as to be present for the removal . . . It would not take long.

Victoria crossed the street in a void, feeling as if she'd lost contact with the earth itself. Ice was so delicate on a June day.

She stood by the door till the long, gray hearse pulled up in front. Two men got out and took a stretcher from the back. A stretcher. No box?

"Are you Miss Seversen?" the older man asked. If he was surprised at her age, he didn't show it.

Victoria nodded.

"Perhaps you would lead the way," he said.

Bicks nodded again. It would not take long. She took them up the stairs. She wondered if the men wore shoes, they walked so quietly, making almost no sound on the steps.

They were gentle, as if the deceased could still feel pain.

75

They covered her with a light, gray blanket. Her face, too. Victoria hadn't thought to cover her face. She could still see the smile.

They left as silently as they had come, as if Mums's body was no burden at all.

They would need a little information for the obituary. It wouldn't take long. Survivors?

A daughter, Victoria, of Dubuque, Iowa.

The man paused. "She can't be very old . . ." He looked at Victoria over his glasses. "The deceased . . ."

"Her mom sent her to live with her aunt. She was too sick . . ."

"I see," said the man. "And you are . . ."

"Her friend. I promised her we'd take care of things . . . since her mother wouldn't let her stay . . . she'll want to know."

"Yes, of course she would. But aren't you a little young . . ."

"My dad had to work or he would've been here. They wouldn't let him off because we're not near relations. You know how it is."

The man nodded, accepting it. Stranger things had happened in this run-down neighborhood, but he couldn't ever recall one so young handling a removal. "Where shall we have the death certificate sent?"

Death certificate? Off guard, Victoria gave Aunt Millicent's name and address. It *did* fit in with her story, after all.

"You plan to attend the services?" he asked.

"Me and my dad," said Victoria. It was no lie. "When . . ."

"We usually prefer a space of three days between the passing on and the services."

Three days!

"To give the survivors time to accept their loss. But since there are no survivors, at least none here . . ."

"No, none," said Victoria.

"And with no visitation or home ceremonies . . ." He stopped. One did not usually discuss such things at a removal, but her

76

presence had unsettled him. "Perhaps I could give your father a call . . ."

"We don't have a phone. But I'd like you to tell me *now* when it'll be so we can get the flowers."

"Thursday," he said. He wondered what her father was like. "What time Thursday?"

"Would your father be able to make it at nine in the morning?"

"Yes, he will," she said. "He's on afternoon shift this week." The lie came so easily. It was as if someone else were speaking for her.

"We don't have a car," she added. "How will we get to the cemetery?"

"It is our policy to provide transportation for the next of kin," he said, "and since you are representing the sole survivor . . ." It was highly irregular! "Perhaps we could . . ."

"That would be just fine," said Victoria. "We'll be there on Thursday. My dad and me. Nine o'clock."

"Nine o'clock." He turned to leave.

"Just one thing," said Victoria.

"Yes?"

"Why don't you use a box?" She had to ask. She couldn't help it.

"A box?"

"The kind for burying." She stopped. That hurt.

"Oh." He looked down at her. "Because it would be indelicate. The bereaved aren't ready to face a coffin at the immediate point of death. You can understand that."

"Yes, I can," said Victoria. She could understand it very well.

The man went down the stairs. Victoria followed him, as if to see him out. What she wanted was one last look, but her will was crumbling and she couldn't manage it. She stood in the doorway, watching, as they drove off.

"Spunky kid," said the younger man as he made a U-turn. No one challenged a hearse.

77

"Never seen the like," said his companion. Something about her disturbed him, but he couldn't pin it down.

Victoria walked slowly up the stairs.

Thursday.

Then she would say goodbye.

Eleven

Stubs waited on the playground for Victoria. He had his address written on a piece of notebook paper. After a while, thinking he'd missed her, he decided to walk on over to her house. It wouldn't take *that* long. He didn't have to fix dinner tonight because Stace was taking him out for burgers, just as if they had all the money in the world. And then Stacey was going to make him spend the five dollars for something he wanted.

Five whole dollars for something he didn't need. Oh, how the wants had flooded in! Something he most particularly didn't need. Whatever he wanted, that five dollars fit. For Stubs, it was a sensation very much like flying.

He rounded the corner, breaking his stick against the mailbox. It made a lovely, hollow whang! And then he saw the hearse.

He gasped for breath and felt cold shivers up and down his spine. The hearse was pulling away and Bicks stood in the doorway looking all crumpled.

He backed off a step, then two steps. It was coming toward him, turning across traffic as if to run him down. He put his hands up in front of his face to ward off the sight. No longer able to stand it, he turned and ran for home as if all hell and its demons were after him.

Stacey came in an hour later and found him huddled on his cot in a corner, quietly crying.

"Stevie," she said, sitting down next to him. She put her arm around his shoulders and drew him toward her. "What's wrong, Stevie? Did someone hurt you?"

Stubs shook his head. "No. No one. I'm not hurt. Only . . ."

"Only what?"

"Only she's dead, Stace. She's dead and Bicks is all alone. And I couldn't even cross the street to tell her how sorry I feel 'cause the hearse was there." He looked up at Stacey, anguish and shame battling across his face. "I couldn't do it. I couldn't. I ran. I couldn't. And Bicks is all alone." He buried his head in Stacey's lap and sobbed.

She didn't understand why the hearse represented such a terror to him, but she accepted the fact that it did, and that he was ashamed of having fled before it.

"She was so good to me. And now she's gone." He grasped Stacey's free hand and pressed it against his chest. "It hurts here," he said.

"Your chest?"

"It hurts so much, Stace. It aches and aches. She wasn't even my mom. Bicks. It must hurt awful for her. Alone and all . . ."

"We'll go to her," said Stacey. "We'll go to her and bring her here. She shouldn't be alone."

Stubs looked up at her. "Can we?"

"Of course we can. She took you in when you needed a place. Now she needs one more . . ."

"She has to go to her aunt."

"Then till she does," said Stacey. "But she shouldn't be alone now." She got up and pulled Stubs to his feet. "You run and wash your face."

"Isn't dirty."

80

"Wash it anyway," she said, "so it won't show you were crying."

"Oh." He went. With Stace beside him he could be brave.

Victoria shut the door and stood alone in the bleak room. It was so empty now, like a vast cavern. The walls seemed to expand until she felt she would fall away in a vacuum.

She couldn't stay here. Of that only was she sure. She would not stay. What, then? Or where? Other decisions eluded her as her thoughts wobbled and wouldn't alight anywhere.

She picked up the newspaper. The one she'd gotten for Mums to read. No one had read it. No one would now. She unfolded it and shook it apart, letting the pages separate and cascade to the floor.

Had she done everything? Was there something she'd overlooked? Her eyes wandered toward the bedroom door. There were Mums's sheets and the blanket. They were good sheets. Someone could use them. *She* didn't want them.

The newspaper rustled under her feet. She went into the bedroom and undressed the bed, folding the sheets and blanket into a loose roll, leaving the bedspread. It was only good for rags. She stuffed the roll into the Goodwill box with a note: "Need washing." She hesitated, then added, "Somebody died on them." Somebody had died.

Wherever she went, she would need food. She went into the kitchen. Bread and peanut butter. She put it into her shopping bag, along with a butter knife and an apple.

The eggs. Five of them. She put them into a pan to boil. Some milk left. She drank it. The grocery money. She would need that for the flowers.

Hard-boiled eggs and salt. It was enough. She looked around. Nothing was left that mattered. She put her key and Mums's key on the table. She left the door open a crack with the latch off.

81

She listened in the hall for a moment, then went quietly down the stairs. The old mattress in the cellar would do for the night. At least this night, and maybe the next.

She paused in the lower hall and looked at the phone. Aunt Millicent was on the other end of it, but she didn't know how to use it. Not for a call that far away. Under her gaze the phone seemed to grow. It became huge and complicated. The slots for coins were like a monster's eyes staring down at her. She fled to the cellar.

It was dark there, but the dark comforted her. She didn't feel so alone in the dark. She took her thin blanket out of the shopping bag and, wrapping it around her, escaped into sleep.

Stubs hurried along with Stacey, skipping, now and then, to keep up. He'd washed his face, but his eyes were still red and his breath caught as it does after tears. There was, in spite of the ache, a tiny bit of gladness in his heart because they were going to help Bicks. She, who'd helped him. She could have his cot. He'd sleep on the floor. And if she didn't feel like going out for a hamburger, he and Stace would fix her supper at their place. And she could stay as long as she wanted.

Even with Stace, he worried about the hearse, and he swallowed hard as they rounded the corner where he'd seen it. But it was gone and he felt stronger.

They waited for the light to change. He wondered what he would say to Bicks when he saw her.

What did you say to someone who'd just lost their mother? Sorry? I'm awful sorry? Stace would know. He didn't. He'd let Stace do the talking. She would know what to say. He reached out and took her hand.

"It'll be all right, Stevie," she said. "You'll see."

They climbed the front steps and went in. They stood for a minute in the dim hall, looking up the stairs, then hand in hand, they slowly mounted them.

82

How would she be? Would she be crying? Was she scared? Would she be glad to see them?

Their feet shuffled in the upstairs hall like feet in church. They reached the door. Stubs saw, at his feet, the ghost of the chalk star Bicks had put there for Stace what seemed a lifetime ago.

Stacey knocked on the door. The sound startled him, though she hadn't knocked loudly. There was no answer.

She tried again. No answer. No sound at all inside. Stace pushed against the door and it opened, creaky on its hinges.

The room was empty. Stacey walked into the bedroom. Striped ticking was exposed on the bare mattress. The bathroom was empty, a ragged towel hanging on the rim of the tub. There were cardboard cartons in the living room, keys on the table, and a shoebox. A newspaper was scattered over the floor.

"She's gone," said Stubs. Why was there always paper on the floor of an empty room?

"Maybe she just went out for a minute," said Stacey. "Maybe if we wait, she'll come back."

"No. She's gone."

"How do you know?"

"The keys," he said, "and this." The shoebox.

She looked at it. His name was printed clear on the box. "What is it?"

"Her cockroaches."

"Cockroaches!"

"She said she was going to send them to someone. To get even, after her mom died. Only maybe she didn't feel like getting even, so she left them for me. 'Cause I liked them." He felt the tears coming. "And I didn't give her anything. I couldn't even say 'I'm sorry.'" He wiped his sleeve across his eyes.

"We'll get her a card," said Stacey. "A sympathy card. And tell her how sorry we feel. And we'll take care of these boxes for her—make sure they go where she wants them to. This one to her aunt's house, and this one to the Goodwill."

It was all they could do. Bicks was gone. They picked up the boxes and left.

Mrs. Jardine had seen them come in from her evening post at the window. She'd recognized Stubs as having been often with Victoria lately. She did not know the person with him. She was too young to be his mother, though she held on to his hand as if she were.

"They're gone," she said, as they came down the stairs. She was well informed if they were not.

Stace set down her box. "Yes, we know," she said. "You haven't seen her, have you? The little girl?"

"Little Purvis? Haven't seen either one of them in days. Heard they went to Iowa to visit a rich relation. Why do you want to know?"

"We came to fetch her," said Stacey, "so she wouldn't be all alone."

"Why should she be alone? She's got a mother to look after her."

"She's dead," said Stacey. She stooped to pick up the box again. "Mrs. Purvis is dead."

"Dead! What do you mean, dead?" She grasped Stacey's arm and stared at her hard to see if she could detect a lie. Purvis was young, skin and bone maybe, but young. It was a shock to Mrs. Jardine and her own mortality. "She can't be dead."

Stacey drew back, not understanding the woman's sudden intensity. "Yes, she is. She must have died today. Victoria . . ."

"What time today?" Mrs. Jardine interrupted.

"We don't know. Stevie here, he saw them take her away."

"Who take her?"

"The men in the hearse. Victoria was here then. But now she's gone. We came to fetch her, but she's gone."

"Where?"

"We don't know for sure. To her aunt's, I guess." Stacey got the door open and followed Stubs out, letting it fall shut behind

84

her. Seemed like every apartment building had a woman like that in it. And the less said, the better.

"Well!" said Mrs. Jardine. She returned to her window and watched the two go up the street. "Least the kid didn't run off and leave a dead body in the house."

She fell to wondering about the boxes the two had carried off and whether there was more where they came from. A half hour later Mrs. Jardine went up the stairs to convey her condolences. She found the rooms empty, as she had expected, and came away with a pair of shoes that pinched her corns, a saucepan, some threadbare towels, the old chenille bedspread, two knives, five forks, and a jar of instant coffee, not more than an inch down. "No sense in having things go to waste," she said.

Twelve

Victoria did not sleep long. She had crept up the cellar stairs to look at her father's watch by the light of the bare bulb hanging over the back door. A little more than five hours. There must be a lot of night left.

But she wasn't tired anymore. At least not heavy tired. She sat on the mattress for a few minutes, then got up and folded the blanket, putting it back in the shopping bag. She groped for her shoes and put them on.

The cellar seemed to quiver in the darkness. The feeble splash of light from the hallway only made it feel more like a pit. She shut her eyes tight to block it out and saw expanding rings of light. The building grew on her mind, threatening. Each brick, each foot of cracked plaster, each splintered floorboard trembled over her, poised to collapse, to crush her. She tried to reason it solid but couldn't. The building was going to fall on her! In panic she fled out the back door and into the night.

The fresh air washing against her face brought her back to reality. She stopped and looked back. The building hadn't fallen in. It was still standing. All the same, she couldn't go back to it. She turned her back to it and went up the alley.

The lilacs. The lilac bushes in Mrs. Edmund's yard. She would be safe under the lilacs. Even if they did fall on her, they wouldn't hurt. She crept under the bushes and wrapped up, once more, in her blanket. The air was good and the leaves rustled in the breeze. They did not smell musty like the cellar, with its odd squeakings and scurryings of mice or, worse, rats. A building like that was bound to have rats. Not that she'd seen any, but she was sure they were there. It was better to be away from them, to be under the lilacs.

Bicks didn't sleep anymore, but waited the night out, trying to steer her thoughts away from her loss. She concentrated on tomorrow, when she would get flowers for the grave. Grand flowers.

She'd never bought flowers before, never even been in a flower shop. Her mind walked her in the door of the only flower shop she knew of. "I'd like some flowers," she said.

"What kind of flowers?"

"Grand ones." No. That wasn't the way. She'd have to act as if she knew what she was doing. Make believe she'd done it before. What were the grand flowers called?

"What kind of flowers?"

"What kind have you got?" No, there was a name for the grand flowers. If she made the right approach, maybe they'd tell her. The kind you bought for Memorial Day. *That* kind of flowers. Would it sound too stupid?

"What kind of flowers?"

"For Mums. You see, she's dead." Bicks's shoulders shook as she fought off the tears.

What had the man said? The one with the hearse. Passed on. That was it. It sounded like being promoted from one grade to the next. Was death a promotion?

"A friend of the family has passed on," she said. A safe way of saying it. Painless. Passed on. "I would like some flowers for

87

the . . . for the . . ." Not funeral. That hurt too much. Burial? No, not that. Grave?

There was a safe word. What was it?

"Some flowers for the . . ." Occasion? Yes, occasion. It sounded cold, but she could say it, and that's what counted. After that it was level ground with practical talk; what type, what price, when, where. "I'll take them with me." She would be determined about that because she didn't want them misdelivered or late. She had to be sure about the flowers. "I'll take them with me."

How much? The grocery money. If it wasn't enough and it might *not* be, well, there was the bus fare. She'd use that if she had to. They'd cost a lot, the grand flowers. But she *must* have them even if she had to walk all the way to Dubuque. She must have the flowers for Mums's grave. Flowers to say goodbye. She *had* to have them.

Tomorrow the flowers.

How much night was left? She wished she'd set the watch correctly. Then she'd know how much night there was. And when to expect the sunrise. The night was so long!

She turned her thoughts to Stubs.

Stacey Martin got up and looked in on her brother. She was angry all over again. Angry with her mother. He'd told her about the cemetery. She hadn't known before. No wonder he'd run for home when he saw the hearse!

He was sleeping peacefully on his cot, one arm thrown across the toy he'd bought that evening. A fuzzy stuffed dog, purple, with a big nose. Maybe it was a little young for him, but he'd never had anything like it before.

They'd carried the boxes home, then gone out for those hamburgers. He didn't seem to want to, but she had insisted. Better that than have him sit home and stew about Victoria when

88

there was nothing they could do about it. He'd tried to perk up. It was an occasion, after all, eating out. But every once in a while a shadow would cross his face and he would shiver all over. He ate all right, though.

There was a discount store down the street. They were walking toward it when he stopped to let a shiver pass.

"What is it, Stevie?" she'd asked. "What's the matter?"

And then he told her about the cemetery. They sat in a doorway and the story spilled out. At the bottom of it was the agony that he hadn't been able to go to Victoria when he'd seen her standing, alone, at the top of the stairs when they took her mother away. He should've been able to. He'd been in a cemetery since, with Bicks, but he couldn't do it.

Stacey hadn't known. She shook with anger. "Sometimes," she said, "it's not possible to be as brave and strong as you want to be. Sometimes you can't do it, no matter how hard you try. This's one of those times. It's not your fault. Don't blame yourself, Stevie. Blame *her*. She was in the way as sure as if she were standing there, in person, between you and Victoria. *She's* to blame, not you."

"You think so," he asked.

"I'm *sure* of it."

There was relief, then. And they'd gotten up and gone into the store. So many things to look at, but he kept coming back to the dog. She wondered if, sometime, he'd like a real dog. Someday, when they could afford it, she would get him a real dog. In the meantime, he was happy with the stuffed toy.

It helped, thinking about Stubs. Victoria could still see him fencing his way down the street with his stick. It warmed her to know he was happy.

She wondered if he'd waited for her after school with his address written down so they'd know where he lived, what he'd

89

done when she didn't show up. She hadn't seen him cover his face and back away. All she'd seen was the dusty gray hearse with the curtains drawn.

She hoped that, somehow, he would get the box of cockroaches and know she'd remembered him. Stubs would get better with Stacey's care. He'd catch up. And, one day, he'd be just as scrappy as any other kid his age. He'd made great progress already. Good old Stubs.

The lilacs were silhouetted black against the graying sky. The night was old at last. Bicks waited for the sun. It came up red, streaking the bellies of the clouds. She wondered if that meant rain. There was a rhyme about red sky at morning. She couldn't quite remember how it went. The clouds weren't that heavy, but they swallowed the rising sun.

She took a hard-boiled egg out of the shopping bag and peeled it, dropping the shell bits into a hollow she'd dug with her heel. She salted it round and round and ate it slowly. Next the apple. It wouldn't keep much longer and she was awfully hungry. A dill pickle would've been nice. She'd left a jar of pickles in the fridge, thinking they'd be too heavy, too awkward to carry. She wouldn't go back for it. A slice of bread. She broke it in pieces and made them into little balls. You could do that with unbuttered bread.

Her breakfast finished, she crawled out from under the lilacs and walked up the alley, away from her former home. She would catch the bus on the next corner. The only flower shop she knew of was next to the cemetery where she and Stubs had put their flowers on the graves before Memorial Day. She would wait in the park until the flowers were ready. No one would notice a kid sitting around in a park *that* much. Kids and parks went together. And there was the shelter house with rest rooms where she could wash up.

A bus came and she got on. Paid her fare. "You wouldn't have the time, would you?" she asked the driver.

90

"Sure do, kid," he said. He consulted his pocket watch. "Not quite half past six," he said, looking at her. "You want it exact?"

"Yes, please."

"I make it 6:28, give or take a second."

Victoria thanked him and sat down. She unbuckled the watch and set it five minutes fast.

"Kinda early for you to be out, isn't it?" asked the driver.

"Got an errand to run," she said, adding, "before school, you see."

"Oh, yeah. School's about out, isn't it?"

"Friday."

"Friday. Bet you'll be glad, huh?"

"Yes," said Bicks.

Six-thirty. It would be a while before the flower shop opened. She decided to ride an extra block and get off across from the park.

The bus slowly filled up. Victoria wondered where they were all going so early in the morning. She sat there listening to the murmur of talk, hearing only the sounds, not the meaning. It was nice to hear voices around her. The night had been so quiet.

"What's that?"

"Rain."

"Can't rain."

"Gonna be a steamer."

"Humidity."

"Don't like it muggy."

"Likely rain by evening." Impersonal, safe talk with strangers.

Victoria got off the bus and crossed the street to the park to wait for the flower shop to open. In the shelter house she washed her hands and face with a wet paper towel. Combed her hair. She looked presentable enough. Later she would change into a dress—for tomorrow.

The shop would open at nine, she decided. Nearly two hours away. She needed a place to wait. The bushes were spiny and

91

caught at her clothes. They wouldn't do. The pines, whose boughs tented down toward the grass, looked inviting, but underneath they were all spiky twigs and pointy needles. All right for hide and seek but not for a long wait.

A shelter of some kind was necessary to her. She didn't know why. She found a picnic table shielded from the street by a row of shrubs. She crawled underneath it and fell asleep. Not that she meant to; it just happened.

Thirteen

"You want to pet my kitty cat?" said a small voice.

Bicks stirred. "What?" she asked.

"My kitty cat. You want to pet him?"

Victoria opened her eyes. For a bewildered minute all she saw was calico fur. She raised her head a little and saw an eager face. A boy of about four had crawled under the picnic table, clutching a cat to show off to her. In spite of being so tightly grasped, the cat seemed philosophical about the situation. It did not struggle.

She put out her hand and patted the cat on its head. It pushed against her hand, purring.

"Why he do that?" asked the boy.

"Because he likes to be petted," said Victoria.

"What about that zipper noise?"

"That's a purr. A cat says he's happy that way." She looked at him. "Are you sure that's your cat?"

There was a moment of doubt. "Sure he's my cat!"

"Where did you get it?"

"Give'm me."

"Who gave it?"

"Cat did. Come up and give'm me. Just like that!"

93

"It's a nice cat," said Bicks, "but it's not yours."

"Is too!" The little face began to crinkle.

"If it was yours, you wouldn't have to hang on to it like that. And you don't know much about cats if you don't know what a purr is."

"Do too! *My* kitty cat!"

Someone called to him and he backed out from under the picnic table, hauling the cat after him, and walked off carrying it mostly by the front end. He was out of sight beyond a pine tree when Victoria heard a shriek.

His mother doesn't like cats, she figured. She was right.

"Marty! Get rid of that mangy beast this instant! Let go of it! Let go, I say!" The scolding voice and the wails grew rapidly fainter as Marty was apparently dragged home for a thorough washing. Poor tyke. He wanted the cat so very much.

Victoria crawled out from her resting place and looked around. The cat was not far off, stalking an unwary sparrow. Bicks whistled and the bird flew off. The cat, thwarted, gave her a look, then trotted off to hunt elsewhere.

"If I was his mom," said Bicks, "I'd give him a kitty cat. But not that one. That's an owned cat with its collar and jingly tags. It belongs to someone . . ." Her voice trailed off.

The flowers! What time was it? Quarter of ten. If it hadn't been for Marty and his kitty cat, she'd still be asleep.

She brushed the bits of grass from her clothes, got out the purse, and took out the grocery money. Folding the bills twice, she put them in her jeans pocket. Then, thinking it might not be enough, she added half the bus fare to Dubuque.

"A friend of the family . . . passed on. I would like some flowers for the . . . occasion." She practiced her words as she walked past the cemetery to the flower shop, feeling a little guilty about the lilacs and the pickle jars. After all, she was on her way to buy *grand* flowers.

She approached the shop timidly. It had such a private look

94

about it. She spent several minutes looking at the things in the window. Fancy vases and flower pots. Ceramic birds and squirrels. Through them she saw a large, glass-fronted case with door handles like a refrigerator. Inside the case were great bunches of flowers in vases like buckets. She recognized roses and carnations, and other flowers she'd seen in the cemetery.

To the left of the case was a small white counter. A woman stood behind it, talking on the phone, writing something down on a pad of paper before her.

In spite of the frightening elegance of the shop and all that was in it, she looked to be an everyday sort of person. The kind you could talk to. She wore a very plain smock like the checkouts at the supermarket and her hair was simply done, not all fussed up.

"A friend of the family . . ."

The woman hung up the phone and went through a doorway behind her into another part of the shop. "Now," Victoria said to herself. She put her hand on the shiny brass doorknob, turned it, and pushed the door open. A bell tinkled over her head, making her jump.

The woman looked in from the back room. She laughed, seeing Victoria's surprise at the bell that still quivered over her head. "We should warn people about that," she said. "It *is* startling when you don't expect it." She had a friendly voice. "Is there something I can help you with?" she asked.

"Uh, yes, there is," said Victoria. "I'd like some flowers." It was coming out wrong.

"What do you have in mind?"

"I don't know," said Victoria. Then, in confusion, "I don't know much about flowers."

"What do you want them for?" the woman asked.

"For a funeral. I mean for a burying. To put on a grave." All those hurting words. "My dad, he said to get flowers, you see. For a friend. Only he had to work."

95

"He should have come himself," said the woman. "Selecting a memorial spray is not a very cheerful task."

The words! She'd said the words! What the grand flowers were called. "Oh, it's all right," said Bicks quickly, "I don't mind. Only I don't know much about flowers. A friend of the family passed on . . ." There. She was saying it right. Passed on. "And my dad said to get the flowers."

Level ground. When? Where?

Why where? "Some cemeteries have restrictions on the types of floral arrangements they allow."

The when. "That's pretty short notice. You'll have to take what we have on hand. There's not enough time to special-order. Now, what did you have in mind?"

Special-order sounded expensive. What did she have in mind? Flowers, of course. Nice flowers. For Mums. What to say next? Victoria had nothing to go on. "Something pretty," she said, "because she was a special friend. Only not too expensive."

"How much were you considering spending?" the woman asked.

How much? Victoria gulped. She was not prepared for that approach. It felt like coming to the checkout at the supermarket and finding you didn't have enough money.

"If you give me some idea," said the woman kindly, "of how much you can spend, then I can show you pictures of what you might get with it."

Oh. Still, it didn't help much. If she said too low a figure, the woman might not take her seriously. And she *was* serious. "Um." She totted up the grocery money in her head, added to it some of the bus fare, to round it off, and gave the woman her total. "Would that do?" she asked.

The woman smiled. "Yes, it will do quite nicely," she said. "With that you can get a very pretty medium-priced spray. Much under that and I'm afraid we wouldn't be able to do

96

much with what we have on hand. Daisies aren't appropriate." She showed Victoria a long, shiny card with various styles of memorial sprays pictured on it, in color. They were all very pretty. Any one of them would make the ache seem less.

After considering them for a long time, during which the woman took two phone orders that amounted to the bus fare to Dubuque and back, Victoria made her choice. "I'd like that one," she said, pointing to it. It *was* grand!

"Oh," said the woman. "I don't know. We're out of lilies because of Memorial Day. We have none in stock." She walked over to the glass-fronted case and looked at the contents. Shook her head. "If you could spare six dollars more, we could substitute mums. The Fuji mums would be beautiful in that arrangement."

Victoria reeled at the word. Mums. Did she know? "Six dollars?" she asked, her voice small and shaky.

"I'm afraid so," said the woman. "The daisies just wouldn't do. Of course, you *could* choose another spray . . ."

"Oh, no," said Bicks. "I want *this* one! I've got the money . . ." Having made up her mind, she couldn't change it. "Only I didn't know there was a flower called mums."

"Chrysanthemums. We call them mums for short. Would you like to see one?" She selected a white flower from one of the containers and held it out to Victoria. It was a large flower with many, many curved petals, some of them much longer than others. It looked like a piece of living lace.

"It's beautiful!" said Victoria.

"Yes, it is," said the woman. "My favorite of the mums. And they last well. Shall I write up the order?"

Bicks nodded.

The woman returned to the counter and got out her order pad. "Name?"

"Victoria Purvis." Not thinking.

97

"And where would you like it sent?"

"Sent? No, I'll take them with me."

The woman frowned slightly. "It'll take a while to make up."

"I can wait," said Bicks. "Or come back for them," she added.

"Well, if you don't mind," said the woman, "but it would be easier to have them delivered."

"Maybe it would," said Victoria, pulling the money out of her pocket, "but I've got to have them with me."

Had she said too much? "You see, it's not a funeral. Just graveside services, and if the flowers are a minute late . . . My dad said . . ."

"All right," said the woman. "Would four o'clock be convenient?"

It would be fine.

Don't pay for them now. Wait until you pick them up. They'll be ready at four.

Victoria left the flower shop. It had been harder to do than she'd thought. You could rehearse your words all you wanted to but, when it came right down to it, they didn't come right. Anyway, it was done. She'd ordered a memorial spray of fire-colored gladiolus and white Fuji mums. It would be beautiful.

She spent the time in between walking around. She didn't dare even sit down for any length of time for fear she'd fall asleep and not go to claim her grand flowers before the shop closed.

She walked through the cemetery and said goodbye to the places where she had set the pickle jars. All the Memorial Day offerings had been cleared away. She went to the park and rested on a swing. You couldn't fall asleep on a swing. She found a little store a block away where they sold sandwiches. She bought a tasteless ham and cheese.

There was an open phone booth outside near the door, the sun glinting off its wary coin slots. Bicks went back into the store. Stranger to stranger, it was easy to ask. How did you make

98

a long-distance call on that phone? As if it were the only one in town that worked.

"Simple," said the clerk. "Put a dime in, dial one and the area code, then the number."

"A dime for long distance?"

"Not on your life! When the call goes through they tell you how much money. You have to put it in before you say hello. It's easier to reverse the charges. Just tell the operator the area code and number. And then if they want to talk to you, they'll pay for it. You're not even out a dime 'cause it comes back."

It made no sense to Bicks. She thanked the clerk and went outside. She didn't have the number anyway. So that phone or any phone might as well have been made out of wood for the use it was to her.

There was a gas station across from the park. Now that the flowers would use up some of the bus fare, she would need a map. She offered to pay for it.

"Naw. They're free," said the man.

She thanked him and left.

She walked once around the cemetery outside the fence. It was three-thirty when she went back to the park and, in the rest room at the shelter house, rolled up her jeans and put on her dress for tomorrow.

Three-forty-five. She said goodbye to the park and walked slowly up the street to the flower shop.

The memorial spray was beautiful. The woman wrapped it carefully to protect it and told her it was best to carry it with the flowers head down. Victoria paid for it and left the shop.

There was still a lot of daylight left. She decided to walk instead of taking the bus. She would spend the night under the lilacs, and was in no hurry to get there. She hoped it wouldn't rain.

At dusk Victoria approached Mrs. Edmund's yard. She sat in the alley with her back against the unused garage until darkness

99

fell. Then she crawled under the lilacs, careful to hang the flowers head down from a branch. She felt that she had managed the day fairly well, had done what she'd required of herself without betraying her feelings to anyone. And then, too tired to eat, she fell asleep.

Fourteen

Victoria woke in the gray hour before dawn and fixed herself a peanut-butter sandwich, then another. She peeled and ate an egg. Mrs. Edmund's garden hose lay across the flower bed. She had a long drink from it, hoping Mrs. Edmund wouldn't hear her. She splashed her hands and face, ran a comb through her hair. It was much too soon but she gathered her things together and walked to the funeral home, carrying the flowers carefully. There were some stairs at the side of the building, bushes shielding both sides. She sat down to wait.

The sun sprang up with a rush, as if it were in a hurry to get the day over with. It was too fast for Victoria, she wasn't ready.

It was a fair morning and would be a fair day. Clouds and rain would have been more appropriate, but the sky didn't mourn for her loss.

She felt all hollow inside as if the least breeze could blow her away. She wanted to huddle on the ground to protect herself. It was with an effort that she sat calmly on the steps, the flowers cradled in her lap. But Mums was in that building at her back. They would have put her in a box by now—a burying box. Bicks sat there waiting to say goodbye.

And she would do it well. She would not cry. Would not, in any way, betray her grief. She would hold herself tightly and they would never know who she really was.

She had disobeyed Mums's wishes. She knew that, but she couldn't help it. She couldn't go away and leave Mums lying there all alone—not knowing when she'd be buried, or, worse yet, whether she'd be buried in the right place with no one to watch. She knew Mums would've understood and felt no guilt for her disobedience. It would've been too hard for her to just walk away as Mums had told her to do. It hurt this way, but it was better.

What would it be like, the burial? A long time ago she'd stood by an open grave, but she couldn't remember the words. She'd been too young to understand. She did remember the emptiness afterward and that Mums had worn black and didn't cry. Not then, anyway. But one night, some time later, Victoria woke to hear her weeping.

Would they let her see her? Or had they nailed the box shut? Would she be able to ask?

For a moment it was hard to breathe. The spell passed quickly with a tremor of denied tears. She would ask to see the body, "for her friend's sake." Insist if she had to. So she could tell Mrs. Purvis's little girl in Dubuque. They would believe her and open the box so she could have one last look. She would *make* them believe her.

What was it like in there? In the building where they had Mums. Was it a nice place? Bicks felt sure it was nicer than the place they'd lived in, where Mums had died. It *had* to be nicer.

She heard sounds in the building—a rattle as the door behind her was unlocked. She jumped to her feet to present a less forlorn appearance. The door did not open. She sat down again. Were the flowers all right? Should she take off the paper? No. Not yet. But soon.

More sounds behind her. As if someone was going around

102

lifting the lids on the boxes to make sure of the dead. And, from the garage at the back, the hum of well-tuned motors being started up. The gray hearse?

"Get a chamois and dust that one off," said a voice. "Got an early run to National."

"Car, too?"

"Yeah."

"Line 'em for escort?"

"Just a minute, I'll check." A pause. "Yeah. Harrison'll be on deck at 8:45. It's to National, after all."

"Right. What's next?"

"Um. Let's see. In-house services at nine. Run to Layman. Must be an old one. Marsden'll be on escort for that. Get the wagon up soon's the National pulls out."

"Didn't know Layman was still open."

"Mostly isn't. Still a few plots left, I hear. Handed down in families. We get about one a year. Hm. Down a quart already. This wagon sure burns oil!"

"They all do. Runs in the breed. What comes after Layman?"

"Nothing scheduled until two. Church gig. That'll leave us two wagons for pick-ups. But look sharp! Tuesday you let a wagon go out with dust on it. I really caught it for that! Never seen Murchison in such a state!"

"Hm. He's generally pretty cool."

"Yeah, well he wasn't about that."

"I'll double check each one I let out."

"You do that." The hood slammed. "It's all yours, Pete."

"Okay."

Bicks stood up and peered over the bushes in time to see the gray hearse driven out of the garage and out of sight at the far side of the building. That was for Mums. Eight-thirty. In fifteen minutes she would unwrap the flowers and walk around to the front of the building, open the door and step inside.

She saw a man return to the garage. That must be Pete, she

103

thought. As he crossed into the garage, he gave a thumbs-down signal.

"Murchison?" asked a voice.

"Yeah," said Pete. "Have to step lively today. He'd fire me for a fingerprint soon's look at me."

"Don't sweat it," said the other man. "He'll be all right after the run to National."

Fort Snelling National Cemetery. That was where Mums would be buried, with her father.

Eight-forty-five. Victoria unwrapped the flowers, folded the paper, put it in her shopping bag. She felt numb all over. A long, gray limousine pulled out of the garage.

It was like sleepwalking, that's what it was. Things loomed up suddenly before her as if they were moving while she stood still. The shrubbery, the short walkway, a flight of five steps glided past her with no effort on her part. She floated, with no sensation of movement, though she knew she left footprints behind her. She felt them though she could not see them.

Bicks stood before the door, wondering if she could open it. It was made of a heavy, dark wood, strap-hinged, like the door of a fortress. It should have a moat before it, she thought, and a drawbridge.

She put her hand on the latch, heard it click, felt the door swing toward her. For all its immense size, it opened easily.

Victoria stepped into a dimly lit, heavily carpeted vestibule and felt as if she'd crossed the threshold into another world where things did not happen, where time did not exist. Everything was muted. Sight, sound, the scent of flowers remembered. There was music, soft and far away. "Nearer My God to Thee." She knew the song and felt comforted by it.

"Miss Sevensen?"

She nodded, seeing no one.

"This way, please."

She found herself following a slender woman down a long

104

corridor with stained-glass windows on one side. Their feet made no sound on the heavy carpet.

Bicks heard a loud snuffle and, turning her head toward the sound, saw a boy not much older than herself standing near a door that opened on the corridor. He held a large, crumpled handkerchief in both hands. Raising it to his face, he saw Victoria.

"My Gramma's *dead*," he said, giving her a look that pushed her away.

A woman stepped into the corridor and put her arms around him. "Come on, Bobby," she said, "it's almost time . . ." Victoria, shaken, turned back to her guide.

"This way, please," she said again. Bicks followed. The sound of crying was swallowed by the stillness of the corridor. They turned a corner and the woman opened a pair of gleaming wooden doors, motioning Victoria to enter.

"Will Mr. Seversen . . ." she began.

"No," said Victoria.

The woman hesitated.

"It's all right."

"Would you like me to stay with you?"

Victoria did not look up at her. "No. Thanks just the same. I'd like to be alone."

The mourner's wishes were respected. The woman left her standing there, alone, in the wide doorway.

For a moment Bicks was unable to move, unable to push herself across the doorsill to her goodbyes. The room was golden lit. The walls, shiny wood. Thick green carpet. A bank of fern. In front of a heavy tapestry was the dark, wooden casket, a rank of lighted candles on either side. The casket was open. She would not have to ask.

She stepped forward, seeing nothing but her mother's face. Everything else fell away except for the terrible pain of saying farewell.

105

She put her shopping bag down and laid the flowers gently on the closed lower half of the casket. She touched the smooth wood, the satin lining, the clasped hands. Remembering touches.

"Goodbye, Mums."

"I came to say goodbye."

"It's me, Victoria." So still. So still. The music. The flowers.

"I love you, Mums." Flickering candles.

"Not yet. Please, not yet." Fern and shiny wood.

"In a little while, Mums. But not yet."

Mr. Murchison came quietly into the room. He saw her standing alone, before the coffin, grasping the rim with both hands. Saw her let go and step back. She raised her head, sensing his presence, and looked around, dry-eyed. "I'm ready," she said.

She picked up the shopping bag and waited for him to lead her away.

He stepped up, as if to close the casket. He stopped, then pulled one of the white mums out of the spray. Victoria watched as he placed it between the clasped hands.

"Thank you," she said.

He nodded without speaking and led her from the room, down the silent corridor, out a side door, and into the limousine. She sat, small, in the center of the wide back seat.

In a few minutes the casket was carried out and placed in the hearse. The little procession began to move. Slowly at first, on the city streets. Then onto the freeway, faster and faster.

They reached the cemetery and the white stones. By the open grave, a grass-like carpet covering the mound of earth, a chaplain waited. He read the service. It was all over so fast.

Victoria stood at the foot of the grave, where they'd placed the flowers. The chaplain across from her. Mr. Murchison and the other man a few paces behind her. The drivers behind them. The policeman by his cycle.

"In my Father's house are many mansions . . ."

"Let not your heart be troubled . . ."

106

"Earth to earth, ashes to ashes, dust to dust . . ."

It was over so fast.

"Miss Seversen?"

"We are ready to return." Gently.

"No. I must wait here. For my dad. He's coming to get me here. He had to work. A friend is driving him. He should be here any minute . . ."

"Are you sure?"

"Yes. I am. Thank you."

"Shall we wait with you?"

"No. Thanks. It'll be all right. He'll be here any minute." He *is* here, she thought.

Mr. Murchison turned, reluctantly, back to the limousine.

Victoria stood straight and still by the edge of the grave and watched them drive away, the chaplain with them. Then she turned back to the grave. Saw only one thing, this grave, this sorrow.

"I'll come back someday, Mums," she said. "I'll come back."

"I don't suppose there're any kids come wandering by with pickle jars . . . Not here, I suppose . . .

"But I'll come back . . . Till then . . .

"The grand flowers . . ."

She knelt and touched the floral spray. Translucent, fire-colored gladiolus. White chrysanthemums. Green fern.

"Keep you safe . . ."

"Know I care . . ."

Victoria stood up with an effort, pulled toward the earth by the open grave. She tried to turn away, then suddenly flung herself down, crouching, with her forehead in the flowers, knees drawn up under her, hands clasped tightly against her lips to prevent the sound from escaping as she fought with her grief and rage.

It had been too much to ask of herself. To turn away calmly, dry-eyed, from her mother's grave required a discipline she did

107

not have; her resolve shattered into a thousand sharp pieces as she wept loudly and long.

After that came peace, or exhaustion; she didn't know which. It mattered little. She began to think of next things. What came after sorrow? It was time to go and she knew it. She rose, unrolled her jeans, tucked the skirt of her dress in at the waist, and picked up her shopping bag.

She walked out of the cemetery, leaving the white stones behind her and the open grave. She did not look back. Time enough to look back another day. In the meantime, she had a journey to begin.

Fifteen

"I don't care what she said about a phone!" Mr. Murchison raged. "One of those Seversens in that book might be a relative! You just keep calling until you find one that knows a girl named Paula! In all my years in this business I've never seen anything like it! Sending a slip of a kid to a funeral all by herself! Pick her up when it's all over!" He sat down at his desk and picked up a pen, tapped it impatiently several times on the desk, then threw it down on the blotter. "I shouldn't have left her there all alone!"

"Paula?" the secretary asked.

"Yes, Paula," he said, getting up. He walked to the window, parted the blind and looked out. "Child abuse! That's what it is! Not four feet tall, and scared. I could tell."

"There's a Paula Seversen listed . . ."

"There's a what?"

"Paula Seversen. In the phone book . . ."

Mr. Murchison crossed the room in two steps and tore the phone book from the startled secretary's hand. She had been delegated to calm him down after the run to National and was having very little success. Fortunately, the in-house service was over and visitation didn't begin for another hour, because all

109

the drapery and thick carpets in the world couldn't muffle the explosions coming from Murchison's office. "Where?" he demanded. "Where?"

She found the place and pointed it out to him.

"Paula Seversen!" he exclaimed. "Surely a relative. An aunt! Has to be! Get her on the phone!"

Mr. Murchison paced the room while she dialed the number. There were a few choice words he'd like to give that little girl's father. He should've waited and met him at the cemetery, but what he had to say he couldn't say in front of her.

The receiver clicked and he stopped. "Well?"

"She's at school," said the secretary, dialing another number.

"School?"

"That's what her roommate said."

"Roommate?"

The secretary shrugged. There was a wait of several minutes; then she handed the receiver to Mr. Murchison.

"Miss Seversen?" he asked. "Miss Paula Seversen?" He paused, identified himself, tried to gather his thoughts. They would not gather. "How could you do it?" he asked. "How could you let her go to a funeral all alone?"

"Let who? What are you talking about?"

"Your namesake. Little Paula Seversen. Couldn't someone have gone with her?"

"Funeral? What funeral?"

"Purvis. Alison . . ."

"Purvis!" Miss Seversen was stunned. "Purvis! Not Victoria!"

"Victoria, Victoria. No. That's the daughter's name. Little Paula . . ." He stopped. Resumed. "Little Paula . . ." No. It couldn't be! "The daughter, Victoria. Do you know her? Could you describe her?"

He listened, seeing her standing before him, the little figure at the foot of the grave. "And I left her out there!"

"Where?"

110

"At the cemetery. National. I'm going out right now and get her." There was no father. Why would she say he was going to pick her up?

"I'll go with you," said Miss Seversen. "Stop at the school. I'll be on the steps."

Mr. Murchison slapped the receiver down, grabbed his hat, and started for the door.

"Where . . ." the secretary began.

"Out to National," he said. "I won't be back today."

"Why . . ."

"The little girl," he said. "Mrs. Purvis was her mother."

Paula Seversen waited at the streetside entrance to the school. Classes were over for the day, the playground deserted.

She had been going through her desk when Mitzi came down from the office to summon her to the phone. Now she knew what had been worrying Victoria and wished, with an ache, that she'd taken the time to talk to her on Monday.

She had been a little concerned at her absence Tuesday, but when she checked with the attendance clerk and heard she'd gone away, she assumed that the worry she'd seen in Victoria's face had been some anxiety about the trip. It did seem odd that they would leave so abruptly when school was nearly over. Could be a relative had died, she had decided, not pursuing it any further.

A relative *had* died, and Victoria had handled everything all by herself. She was not surprised. Victoria was bright and resourceful and had a tough resilience that few ten-year-olds or adults could match.

"Miss Seversen?"

She looked up. A grandfather in a little orange car. "Mr. Murchison?" He nodded. She got in, and he headed for the nearest freeway entrance.

"I had a strange feeling about it right from the first," he said,

111

shaking his head. "But she was so *convincing!* Friends of the family, she said. Her dad was at work."

He shook his head again, remembering. "You should have seen her eyes when she turned away from the casket. How could I not have guessed then? That haunted look. I've seen it before. She turned to me from the open casket. 'I'm ready,' she said. That was all."

They reached the cemetery. A grounds keeper was placing sod on the freshly filled grave, the flowers lying brightly near the white stone. Purvis. Thomas.

"Where is she?" Murchison asked.

"Who? The little girl?"

"Yes. The girl. Have you seen her?"

The man shook his head. "No. Not in a while." He straightened up and looked off across the cemetery. "I come to fill the grave," he said, "and I seen her crouching here, cryin', so I go away for a while, till she's cried herself out.

"When I come back, she's gone. I said a 'Hail Mary' over the flowers before I moved 'em. Ain't seen her since."

They returned to the car. "Maybe someone *did* pick her up," said Paula. "Maybe a friend . . ."

Mr. Murchison looked at her bleakly. "You'd think if she had a friend they would have come to the funeral with her."

She nodded. "Yes, you would think that. But she must have had some way of leaving here; otherwise, she would have returned with you."

"It's possible." He thought for a minute. "She might have just gone home . . . But there was that shopping bag . . ."

"Maybe she was going to stay with someone."

He started the car. "We can check back at her apartment. That's the only thing I can think of right now. I shouldn't have left her here!"

"Don't blame yourself. You didn't know . . ."

112

"But I should've guessed. Old Barney's not known to be delicate about graves and probably never thinks to say a prayer over them. He's got his grounds to keep and a clock to punch, and that's all that matters to him."

"Let's try her house first," said Paula, "and then, if she's not there, perhaps we could check with her friend Steven Martin. He might know . . ."

"Close friend?"

She nodded. "I think so. All the past week, the one before this, they came and went together. She seemed to be kind of watching over him. As if he'd had some trouble."

"Know where he lives?"

"No. But we can stop at the school and find out."

The apartment was drear and empty. Paula looked around. Victoria had faced death all alone in that awful place. "The keys . . ." she said.

"Yes, I see them. She didn't mean to come back here, then." He sighed heavily. "The boxes are gone, too."

"Boxes?"

"She had two boxes just here," he said, pointing, "by the door." He dropped his hand in a gesture of helplessness. "Why didn't I *realize?*" He turned to Paula. "She was so *earnest!* So *convincing!*"

"She must have meant for you not to guess who she was. She wanted it that way. Why, I don't know."

"Neither do I. At least I did *something* for her. The escort and the viewing. At least I did that."

They left the door ajar, as they had found it, and descended to the street where Mr. Murchison had parked his car. Mitzi was just leaving school when they arrived, but found Steven Martin's registration card for them, the address only a few blocks from where Victoria had lived.

A few minutes later they were walking slowly up the rickety

113

stairs to the third floor back, where Stubs had lived. If anything, it was worse than the building they had just left. The halls were sour, airless, cracked; peeling wallpaper, weeping ceilings.

Miss Seversen knew that many of her students lived in places like this, but it was numbing to have it brought home to her. She never visited the homes, and the parents rarely visited the school. It was a giving-up way to live. No wonder it was so hard to get them to respond. Victoria had been an exception, though seeing how she'd lived, she wondered why.

The woman that answered their knock seemed furtive. As if she had something to conceal. She stepped out into the hall, pulling the door to behind her. But her eyes kept wandering toward it as if something on the other side needed watching. There was something in her manner that made Paula think of a beast of prey tensing for the kill. It came unbidden to her mind and she couldn't shake it off.

At first she said she *was* Beulah Martin. In the next breath denied it. When they asked about the boy, her hand tightened on the doorknob and her right shoulder twitched toward the room behind her.

She released the knob and backed slowly into the room, her eyes on Mr. Murchison, a look of stunned horror, not of him but of herself, Paula thought. He advanced toward her as if she drew him with her.

They stood there for a moment, staring at each other, and then the animal in her struck. Just quick enough to ward off her blows, he grabbed her wrists and tried to force them down.

"The boy. Look for the boy," he said.

Paula slipped past them into the apartment and looked quickly through the rooms, calling for Steven. Saw what the woman hid. The violence she had visited on the place. Furniture, clothing, bedding, dishes, food. Ripped, broken, slashed, burned, scattered.

Mrs. Martin began to scream imprecations. Her strength rose

114

with her voice and Mr. Murchison had all he could do to hold her.

"Beulah Martin!" Paula shouted. "Stop that!" As if she were causing a disturbance in class.

It worked. Beulah Martin went limp and nearly fell. She staggered back a few paces, then slumped to the floor. She sat in the shards and splinters, sat rocking and weeping in the wreckage.

"Poor Beulah," she whimpered. "Oh, poor Beulah. Killed her baby, she did. Poor Beulah."

Mr. Murchison watched her for a moment. Shook his head in pity. He looked from her to Paula. A question. She nodded. He helped the woman to her feet and they guided her, one on each side, down the stairs, out the door, and into his car.

"Poor dead baby. Poor Beulah." All the way to Hennepin County Medical Center, tears and poor Beulah, poor baby, poor Beulah. They got her in the door of Emergency before the rage returned. They knew how to handle it there. She would get the treatment she needed.

Mr. Murchison drove Paula home. "About the boy," he said, "do you think he's still alive?"

"Yes, I'm sure of it. After whatever happened there, he must have gone to Victoria's. That explains her watching over him as she did. I'll leave a note with his teacher tomorrow, telling her I want to see him."

"I'll be there," he said.

115

Sixteen

Victoria stood below the rim of the hill and looked back across the Minnesota River and the stone arches of the Mendota Bridge. So high, the bridge, but so small from where she stood. Back toward where she knew the cemetery to be, though she could not see it. And farther back yet, to where the sun was slowly sinking into a bed of cloud. The western sky was red and gold, with pink higher up, shimmering and echoing back from the river.

It was like watching a great anthem, but instead of hearing the music, she saw it. She felt a hush fall on the grasses around her. It reminded her, somehow, of the Easter service they'd gone to, she and Mums, when they'd waited in silence for the sunrise. And when the sun raised the colors of the great stained-glass windows, the choir had sung "Christ Is Risen" with such joy she'd been moved to tears. She'd tried to hide them, but she saw that Mums's cheeks were wet, too.

The sunset was like that moment, only higher and freer. Not hemmed in by walls of stone. It rose up and up to a point of golden light that faded slowly. Bicks watched the land grow dark all around her and the river turn white in the starlight.

She wrapped herself in her blanket and lay down in the tall

116

grass to sleep. She had seen it through and it had all been done properly. Her mother and father rested together in the quiet green cemetery. They were together somewhere else, too. She was sure of it.

A dog barked far away. Stray dogs and the weather. She was too tired to worry about it. She slept.

The sun had been up a long time before she woke again. She stretched and yawned, feeling soft and rested, and very hungry. She would eat a real breakfast in the café across the highway and then set out on her journey. That would give her two empty milk cartons to carry her water in when there were long miles between gas stations or stores.

Her meal the day before had been all that hunger could desire. A great big greasy hamburger with all kinds of green stuff on it. What had the waitress said? "Through the garden." That was it. And french fries and milk in a carton.

After her breakfast, she would be more careful with her money so it would last. But right now she needed to eat.

Eggs and toast. Milk and orange juice. She studied the road map while she ate and added the miles in her head. There weren't that many. At least, considered as numbers. Step by step it might seem longer. But she welcomed the prospect: to walk all day in the sun and wind until she was too tired to grieve and sleep was deep and dreamless.

Five days to Rochester, she figured, unless the weather turned bad. Rain would slow her down. If her money was enough, she would take the bus from there. If not, well, walking was free.

She washed her face and brushed her teeth in the rest room of the café. She changed into her oldest jeans and a cotton knit shirt. She took her windbreaker out of the shopping bag, wrapped the photo album in the dress she'd worn to the funeral, and repacked the bag, wedging the milk cartons full of water firmly in place on top so they would not tip and spill.

She brushed her hair, then wound it up and tucked it under

117

an old baseball cap. It had been too big, but with her hair pushed into it, it fit quite snugly. She was ready to go.

Bicks left the café and started up the long hill, walking on the left side of the road, facing traffic, the way you were supposed to when there weren't any sidewalks.

It was a beautiful day. The wind was at her back and there were little scudding clouds. The sun was warm. After a while she took off her windbreaker and tied it, by the sleeves, around her waist.

She set an even pace, changing hands with the shopping bag every fifth telephone pole. After every fifth change she would climb down the grassy edge of the road to rest for five minutes. Tomorrow she promised herself ten-minute rests, but today, since she'd gotten a late start, five would have to do. The little goals added up, and by sundown, she'd reached the town of Coates.

She was stiff and tired and very, very hungry. She bought a hamburger to go at a little tavern, not caring what it cost, and crept off the road into a field at the outskirts of the town. She settled down on the far side of a graying haystack and forced herself to eat slowly, though her hunger demanded immediate satisfaction.

When she'd licked the last of the good tastes from her fingers, she peeled and ate one of the remaining eggs and drank the last of her water. She'd noticed a standpipe with a faucet outside the tavern and figured she could refill the cartons early in the morning when there'd be nobody around.

She curled up and went to sleep with her back hard against the haystack. The gray of her blanket blended in with the weathered hay, and even in the bright moonlight, she was hardly to be seen.

Mr. Murchison waited in the hallway while Paula dismissed her students and was nearly trampled in the rush for summer.

118

It had been a long time since he'd been in a school, but it still smelled the same. Of chalk dust and, even now, wet mittens, of washroom soap and wet paper towels, of red soup, tempera paint, library paste.

The hall emptied in seconds. He entered the classroom. Paula was erasing the blackboard for the last time. He could still see the words, "Have a nice summer."

There was a small sound at the door. Not quite a cough. He looked down at the boy, Steven Martin. Short, dark-haired, thin, he appeared pale under the freckles and a little apprehensive.

Paula smiled at him and asked him to come in. Told him Mr. Murchison was a friend and he shouldn't be afraid.

The boy eased into the room and sat at one of the desks. Miss Seversen sat on the desk in front of him.

"Steven," she said, "we are looking for Victoria Purvis. Her mother died . . ."

"I know," said Stubs. "Me and Stace, we went over there Tuesday to get her to come stay with us. Only she was gone."

"Tuesday?" asked Mr. Murchison.

"Yuh. See, I went over after school Tuesday to give her my address and there was the hearse just pulling away and I . . . and I ran scared for home. Stace, she could tell you why. But we went back later and she was gone. Left some boxes all addressed so we took care of them for her. Since we couldn't take care of her . . ."

"Stace?" asked Paula.

"My sister. I live with her."

"Your mother?" asked Mr. Murchison.

"She don't want me," said Stubs. "Don't want none of us." It still hurt. "Bicks. Uh, Victoria. She and her mom, they took me in after . . ." He sighed, sharply. "Stace, she come and got me."

"Did she hurt you much, your mother?" asked Paula.

119

Stubs looked at her, surprised. "How . . ."

"We've seen her," she said, "and from what she told us, we were afraid she'd hurt you. I'm glad to see you're all right."

"She didn't mean to," he said. "It just comes on her sometimes like that. Just comes on . . ." He paused, looked from one to the other. "She all right?" he asked.

"We took her to a hospital," said Paula gently, "where she'll get the care she needs."

Stubs looked down at his shoes. "She's crazy, isn't she." It was not a question. He didn't need an answer.

Paula changed the subject. "You haven't seen Victoria since Tuesday?" she asked.

He shook his head.

"We'd hoped she'd gone to you after the funeral. That you could tell us where to find her."

"Funeral?"

"Yesterday."

"But she shouldn't have. Her mom told her to leave right after she died."

"She didn't," said Mr. Murchison. "She stayed. Where, I don't know. She bought flowers and went to the graveside service alone. I didn't know until afterward who she was. She gave Miss Seversen's name and said she was a friend of the family. I left her out there in the cemetery. When I found out who she was, we went back to get her, but she was gone."

"She went to her aunt's," said Stubs. "On a bus. Anyway, she was supposed to. Had bus money. Her mom planned it that way, not to cause trouble for anyone."

"Are you sure of that?" asked Mr. Murchison.

"Don't know where else she'd go," said Stubs.

"Where does her aunt live?" asked Paula.

"Iowa somewhere. Got a 'Q' in it."

"You wouldn't know her name?"

120

"Aunt Millicent."

"I mean her last name."

"Same as Bicks's. Purvis."

"Purvis," said Mr. Murchison, "of course! The information for the death certificate. I've got her address at my office. Let's go over there and call her!"

"Can I go now?" Stubs slid out of the seat and edged toward the door. He'd been putting things together and had arrived at the conclusion that the old man with Miss Seversen was in the burying business, which was appalling, however nice he seemed.

"Wouldn't you like to be with us when we call Victoria's aunt?" asked Paula.

"Can't," said Stubs. "Got work to do."

"Then we'll give you a ride home," said Mr. Murchison.

Stubs would rather have walked, but he couldn't figure out how to refuse a ride without sounding stupid. He was awfully glad the old man's car was little and orange and not big and black and scary.

As they drove along, he explained what work he had to do. He needed to wash the dishes and make the beds and fix supper for Stace because she would be tired when she got home after working and going to school.

"How old is she?" asked Mr. Murchison.

"She's sixteen," said Stubs, "only we're pretending she's older so she can keep me with no one making a fuss."

"Do you need any help?" asked Mr. Murchison.

"Help? No. Me and Stace, we're all right. Got all we need and each other besides." The way he said it, it sounded as if he owned the world. Mr. Murchison decided he would have to meet the boy's sister. That, and offer her any aid she might accept. He found out where she worked and Miss Seversen wrote down their home address.

"If you get to talk to Bicks," said Stubs, safely out of the car,

121

"tell her me and Stace sent the box to her aunt. Stace, she washed the sheets and stuff before we took it to the Goodwill. She'd want to know."

He watched them drive away, feeling awfully tall and brave considering he'd ridden in a car with a burying man and not showed how scared he felt. Then he went out to pick some weeds in the alley to decorate their supper table.

Millicent Purvis hurried home from work Friday night. She had many things to do. Though she'd had no letter from them, she expected her sister-in-law and her niece, Victoria, to arrive sometime during the weekend and she wanted things to be just right.

There were the new curtains for Victoria's room to be hung. And the four-poster bed in Alison's room would need polishing. The rugs had been cleaned, the dresser drawers lined with fresh paper. Groceries. She must be sure to get some peanut butter for Victoria. And what else? Something for a special treat. She took her mail out of the box, checked it briefly. Nothing in Alison's hand. She tossed it on the dining-room table and went out to the kitchen to make a list. Strawberries. If there were nice strawberries at the store, she would make a shortcake.

What if they came while she was gone? She stopped halfway out the door. It wasn't impossible to expect them this soon. But Alison would remember where she hid her extra key. She chalked a note of welcome on the kitchen blackboard and hurried off to the store.

When she returned she put away the groceries and set the strawberries on the sink to be cleaned later. The curtains first. They would need pressing. She set up the ironing board in Victoria's room so she could hang each panel as soon as it was ironed. Such pretty curtains. Victoria would like them, she was sure.

122

When she was finished, the room looked so warm and friendly, it was hard to believe she was the only one in it. She sighed. "Tomorrow, then," she promised the waiting room. "Tomorrow."

She polished the four-poster, then went downstairs to clean the strawberries. For once there were few imperfections. She put them in a covered glass bowl and set them, weeping in sugar, in the refrigerator.

After a cold meat-loaf sandwich and a glass of buttermilk, she set about dusting the spotless downstairs room, then rearranged the books she'd gotten for Victoria, putting her favorite on top. They were paperbacks, lovingly selected. They would provide her with entertainment until she made new friends. She could hear the shouts and laughter of the one last game before dark. It made the quiet room seem all the quieter.

Millicent stood in the darkening room, fingering the lacy afghan she'd crocheted for Victoria's mother to wear against the evening mists. Though she lived up on the bluff where the river mists couldn't reach, she firmly believed that one needed protection from them, especially one as frail as Alison.

She roused herself and continued her dusting. The mail was on the dining-room table. A bill. A magazine. A couple of ads. She was about to put them away in the breakfront when one of the envelopes seemed to leap up at her. She stared at the return address for a moment, and she felt suddenly cold. She opened the envelope, her hands shaking so badly she nearly tore it in half.

"Oh, my word!" she gasped. "Oh, my word!"

A death certificate.

Alison was gone.

And Victoria? Where was *she*? Millicent looked around the room as if she expected the walls to answer. The quiet settled around her. After a few minutes she realized she was crying. Crying for Victoria's loss and her own.

123

Alison had always been delicate, but there'd been no clue she was near death. Not from Victoria, anyway. She'd just talked to her not a week ago. Something about a friend staying with them and being almost out of Kleenex. It hadn't made much sense, Victoria'd explained it so fast.

A cold. She looked at the death certificate. No, it wasn't that. She'd died on Monday. Victoria had been all alone ever since.

Millicent placed a call to Minneapolis.

Purvis was dead and the kid had gone to live with an aunt in Iowa somewhere.

"When?" asked Millicent.

"When what?" asked Mrs. Jardine.

"When did she leave for Iowa?"

"How would I know? All I know is, the kid's gone and the place is for rent. Or will be soon. Cleared out, she did, without so much as a decent goodbye."

"Are you sure she went to Iowa?" asked Millicent, wanting to shake the woman on the other end. Shake her for being so hard and uncaring.

"I'm not sure of nothing," said Mrs. Jardine. "But she talked some of an aunt in Iowa and going to visit her. And her friends, they knew she'd gone . . ."

"What friends? Who?"

"Runty-looking kid. Boy. And an older girl. Came after she'd gone. They took some boxes. Stole them for all I know. I'd seen him around some, but not to know his name. Standoffish, if you catch my meaning."

"I don't," said Millicent, "but if you see them, would you ask them to write to me?" She gave her name and address.

"You the aunt?" asked Mrs. Jardine. "Kid hasn't showed, huh? Well, I wouldn't worry none. Little Purvis can take care of herself. Independent as they come. Not sassy-like, mind, but

124

keeps herself to herself. She's a cool one, little Purvis. She'll show up. You can count on that!"

"I hope so," said Millicent. "I hope so." She hung up and sat for a few minutes staring helplessly at the phone. There was no one she could think of to call at this late hour in an attempt to locate Victoria. The office that sent the death certificate would be closed, and even if it wasn't, they wouldn't be likely to know where she was. But they might be able to tell her who had handled the arrangements. There was a remote possibility that someone at the funeral home would have some idea of what had happened to her niece.

"Monday," Millicent said softly. "Monday. She would've stayed for the funeral. At least, I would think so."

She wished she'd been more persistent on the phone. Even if that woman hadn't actually seen Victoria leave, she might have some notion of when. And the friends who seemed to know where she was going. Assumed, in fact, that she'd gone. When had they appeared? What day? She thought briefly of calling the Minneapolis Police Department, but dismissed it. She was with her friends, of course. They had missed connections earlier, but now, she was sure, had found each other. Victoria was *not* alone, she was with those friends.

The funeral. It wouldn't have been on Monday or Tuesday. That was too soon, or it seemed, to her, that it would be. Wednesday? Thursday? Maybe even as late as Friday. Today was Friday. If it was today, she might be on her way right now. On the bus. She'd said they had the bus fare.

Millicent called the depot and found that the bus was expected in twenty minutes, though it had lost an hour on the way. The one that had connections from the Twin Cities. She drove down to meet it and watched as sixteen rumpled, weary people stumbled down the bus steps. Victoria wasn't among them. She turned away. Tomorrow, then. Perhaps she'd been

125

too tired or too sad to set out today. Perhaps . . . The thought would not obey her wish to leave it unconsidered. Perhaps Victoria had lost her bus fare and was somewhere alone, hungry and frightened, not knowing where to go for help.

The friends. The boy and the girl. She was with them. Surely she was!

Seventeen

Buttercups glowed brightly through the fog. Bicks stirred and sat up. A striped gopher streaked away through the grass and disappeared. Six a.m. She wound the watch, ate the last of the eggs, and wished for some jelly to go with her peanut butter. She promised herself that the next time she spotted a store, she would get some.

She shook her blanket, folded it, and put it in the shopping bag. Washed her face and hands at the standpipe and filled her milk cartons. Set her goal for the day. She would not stop until she reached it: one inch on the map. Farther if she wasn't too tired. There was little traffic at that hour.

She ate peanut butter and jelly for lunch and drank a whole quart of milk. She had bought a packet of beef jerky, too, though it was expensive. She felt guilty about spending so much money all at once. At the rate she was going, she would not be able to take the bus at Rochester. When she was tired she could rest, that was free, but when she was hungry she had to eat. And that cost money.

The hunger was with her all the time—a mean, gnawing hunger. She felt that it was somehow related to her tears, to her sorrow. The greatest feast would not defeat it, only time. It did not occur to her that in walking through all the daylight hours she needed more food than she normally would have.

The fog lasted the whole day. In fact, it seemed to deepen as evening drew on. Once someone offered her a ride. She refused, politely, saying she didn't have far to go. It was true—an inch a day was not far. Sixteen miles to an inch. She figured she'd done a little better than that when she stopped for the night.

She would have looked no farther than the roadside ditch, but it was wet at the bottom. She scrambled up the low bank on the other side and crawled under some low-growing brush, too tired to eat. She wrapped up in her blanket and went to sleep.

Sunday. Victoria ate the packet of beef jerky and walked all day in a light but steady rain. She bought a loaf of bread, some cheese already sliced, and an apple. Such a wonderful apple! She ate it right down to the skeleton, then planted the seeds beside the road. Maybe they'd grow, and someday, someone walking along as she was would find an apple tree there with apples on it free for the taking.

That night she took shelter in a tumbled, abandoned house not far from the highway. Had she been much bigger it would not have served, for the roof took up most of the space inside. It had fallen in an orderly fashion as if it had been picked up and inverted by a giant hand.

She was glad she'd found it. The rain was falling harder and the wind had begun to blow in gusts. Her clothes were only damp, the earlier rain had been so light—more like a heavy mist. She removed her shoes and shirt and felt the envelope pinned to her undershirt. It was all right, she decided. She put on a dry shirt and hung the damp one from a splinter of wood that stuck out of the wreckage. She was glad of the heavy plastic bag that protected her things. She ate her supper sitting with her back against the front wall of the house, not far from

128

the door, in case she had to leave in a hurry. The timbers groaned and creaked around her as the wind got stronger, but the front wall barely trembled. She decided to trust it.

Bicks was jolted out of sleep by a loud crash. She sprang up, bumping her head on the caved-in roof. "It's thunder," she said, "only thunder." She sat down again and listened. Hail rattled against the walls and rolled down the roof. Lightning flashed green and the thunder shook the earth all around. She was not alone. In the flashes of lightning she could see that a pair of rabbits had taken shelter in the far corner along the wall, huddled together, ears flat. Perhaps they had been flooded out of their burrow. She sat perfectly still so she wouldn't frighten them out into the storm.

The sun was shining brightly when Victoria opened her eyes. The rabbits were gone. She sat on the crooked steps in front of the ruined house and made herself a peanut butter with jelly and cheese. The world seemed so bright and clean around her that it was hard to believe the violence of the night. And even harder to understand how the jumble of boards had stood up to the storm. Had she seen it in clear light, she would never have considered sheltering there.

The day was already hot. She would have to ration her water. After breakfast, she figured she had barely a cupful left. It would be noon before she reached the next dot on the map, and she would have to cut her rest periods to do even that.

But the noon hour came without that dot. She passed a farm or two with pumps in their yards, but she couldn't make up her mind to trespass. The pumps probably didn't work anyway. Twelve-thirty. One o'clock. Finally she saw a dark clump of trees through the heat shimmer and knew it must be a town. She drank the last of her water and quickened her pace.

Her plan was to find a gas station, fill her cartons, and keep right on going. She didn't reckon on her nose. It led her, re-

129

sisting every inch of the way, to a little café that offered HOME COOKING in big letters on the window. Past the lunch hour, the place was deserted. The special was chalked on a blackboard behind the counter: *Beef Stew*. She ordered it. It smelled so wonderful she was helpless to deny herself. She got the very last serving with a little extra, the good brown scrapings from the bottom of the pot.

Victoria tried to eat it slowly, to make it last longer, but she couldn't manage it. Too soon, the plate was empty. She would have licked it clean but felt the waitress watching her.

She got up and went to the rest room, where she washed her face and filled her water cartons. She walked through the café on the way to the door.

The waitress was erasing the blackboard. She turned as Victoria went by. "Say, kid," she said, "you forgot your dessert."

"Huh?" There'd been nothing about dessert on the menu.

"Your dessert. Here," she said quickly, "you can take it with you if you're in a hurry." She took two big apple turnovers from the case above the counter and, wrapping them in a napkin, thrust them into Victoria's hand.

Bicks was stunned. "Gee," she said, "gosh, thanks!"

The waitress smiled a little crookedly. "One's the usual," she said, "but you look like you could use two."

"Oh, thank you!" said Victoria. "Thank you!"

"Don't mention it," said the woman, turning back to the chalkboard. Dismissed, Victoria left the café. The waitress watched her walk by the window and out of sight, carrying the turnovers carefully, as if they were beyond price. "Can't stand to see a kid that hungry," she said softly to herself.

She took some of her tip money from her apron pocket and rang up the price of the turnovers.

Victoria walked until sunset, carrying the beautiful turnovers in her shopping bag. She'd bought a pint of milk at a little store and planned to make her supper of apple turnovers and

130

milk. She felt stronger for the stew and, by the end of the day, had put nearly twenty miles between herself and the pile of broken boards where she'd spent the night.

She found a little grassy ravine with stunted apple trees growing up its slopes and there made her bed. The milk was warm but not sour and the turnovers were wonderful! The night came clear and mild, and her sleep was undisturbed.

Toward morning the stars winked out, one by one, as clouds rolled in to hide them. When Bicks woke the sky was white with a solid overcast. Too high and light for rain. It was cooler than the day before, which she appreciated.

She made a peanut butter and jelly sandwich, then got out Mums's purse to count her money. Just touching the purse brought back the ache that she had held off so well in the weariness of the past few days. The note. She hadn't read it yet. She wouldn't now. When it was all behind her, she would read it.

The money wasn't as much as she expected, even adding what she carried in her jeans pocket. She counted it again. The same. Had she lost some? Or had she spent more than she calculated? Would it be enough? She decided that when she got to the outskirts of Rochester she would find a phone booth and call the bus depot. A dime one way or the other surely wouldn't matter much. And if she didn't have enough, it would be less embarrassing. There was a lot of difference in being poor in person and being poor over the phone.

It was Tuesday. A week ago she'd stood alone on the front steps and watched them take her mother away. It seemed like a hundred years. Bicks cried for a while, just a little while. Then she gathered up her things, wiped her face on her sleeve, and set out. There were many miles ahead of her.

She did not stop for lunch but nibbled at the cheese as she walked. Still, it was all but five o'clock by the time she reached Rochester and five-thirty before she found a phone booth.

131

She was more than two dollars short. "That much?" she asked, dismayed.

"Yeah," said the voice. "Rates went up all across the board first of the month to catch the summer traveler."

Two dollars. If she had to walk farther she would have to spend more for food. The peanut butter was nearly gone. She'd eaten the last of the bread for breakfast. There was the jelly. But you couldn't live on jelly and walk all day.

She checked the stops on her bus schedule and marked them on the map. More than two dollars! A loaf of bread and some peanut butter would eliminate the first stop. She was pretty sure of that. And, maybe, the next.

Two more days at the least, then. She found a store and made her purchases. Asked the clerk about city buses.

"Crosstown's due any minute. Catch it if you hurry. Last express run of the day. Get it up on the next block. Wish they ran 'em later. Wouldn't drive if they did."

Bicks ran for it. If she caught that bus, then she could get clear of the city before it was quite dark. She didn't want to spend the night there. It had been different sleeping under Mrs. Edmund's lilacs. That, at least, was home, or very near it. This was not.

She reached the stop just as the bus pulled up. It was nearly full and the driver was arguing baseball trades with some of his regulars. No one paid much attention to her.

She got off at the end of the line and watched as the bus turned around and headed back into town, taking its light and sound with it, leaving an empty quiet behind. She walked on for nearly a mile before looking for a place, off the road, to spend the night. She found a level spot among the tall weeds by the roadside and spread out her blanket for a pretend picnic. It helped to make her meal seem special, though she was sick to death of peanut butter.

It was some consolation, though, that she might not have

132

been able to take the bus from Minneapolis as she was supposed to because the ticket price had gone up. They hadn't thought of that, she and Mums. She told herself she would have walked a lot farther just for those beautiful flowers.

She turned her thoughts away from the hurt to other things. Stubs, what was Stubs doing tonight? She remembered the day his lunch ticket had been stolen and how he'd nearly choked on the peanut butter she'd given him. "Bet he's eating better to-night," she said.

Another peanut-butter sandwich. She drank some water, wrapped up in her blanket, and fell asleep. Her dreams were of food. Fried eggs and buttered toast. Tuna-salad sandwiches. Pizza. Anything but peanut butter!

Eighteen

Millicent found Victoria's box on her front porch when she got home from work Tuesday. There was a note inside from Stacey telling how they'd found it in the empty apartment and sent it on to her because that was all they could think of to do for Bicks.

She carried it up to Victoria's room and began to unpack it. The things in the box were so worn and shabby she wondered why she'd bothered to pack them at all. Had they been that poor? Millicent put the things back in the box and went out to buy a few replacements. Pajamas, a robe, some pretty underwear, though it didn't seem reasonable to do so. She had the box, but Victoria had disappeared as if she'd been swallowed by the earth. No one had seen the little girl in the blue dress since the caretaker at the cemetery let her have her cry before he filled the grave. They had searched the cemetery and the area all around it but they'd found no sign of her. There was no clue as to what had happened to her.

Mr. Murchison had assured her that, even though the police were no longer actively searching for her, they did have bulletins out describing Victoria. Surely, sooner or later, she would be found. All they could do was wait and hope.

She took her purchases up to Victoria's room and put them

away. The phone rang and she jumped. It was the ticket agent at the bus depot. The evening bus was in. There was no little girl on it. He'd call again tomorrow.

She read the letter from Miss Seversen. She'd sent her Victoria's report card. Her grades were very good. Promoted to the sixth grade. The letter was encouraging, or meant to be. But, behind the words, Millicent felt little hope. She sighed and put the letter away. She would try to write to Miss Seversen on Saturday or Sunday, at Camp Courage, where she worked for the summer, to thank her for her concern and the report card.

If Victoria was dead, they'd at least have found her body by now. She thought of the river and shivered. They hadn't searched the river. She had asked Mr. Murchison about it and he told her that the authorities considered it unlikely. Had she been spotted near the river, perhaps they would've tried dragging for her body. But no one had seen her there.

It had been nearly a week since Alison's burial, since Victoria was last seen. She had talked to Mr. Murchison twice. He had called on Saturday and again on Monday. They had tried to reach her on Friday but she'd been at work. He felt sure, in spite of the failure of the search, that Victoria would be found. Though where she was now, he couldn't say. He went, each day, to the cemetery, early in the morning, and waited by Alison's grave to see if Victoria would return. When the flowers faded he got new ones. He based his hopes on the calm strength she had shown in the face of shattering sorrow.

Millicent, in spite of his confidence, dwelled mostly on the words of Mrs. Jardine: "Little Purvis can take care of herself." They ran through her mind a thousand times a day. "Little Purvis can take care of herself." The tone, so scornful, as if only a fool would worry.

Through Mr. Murchison she learned about Stubs and his sister. And how certain Stubs was that Victoria was on her way to Dubuque, though he couldn't explain the delay. Little scraps

135

of hope bunched together. She clung to them like water wings in a swift current.

The phone again. Mrs. Lacey across the street. She kept an eye on the house during the day in case a little girl in a blue dress showed up on the front porch. She had a daughter Victoria's age and kept a mother's vigil.

"Maybe tomorrow," said Mrs. Lacey, wishing her news was better.

"Or the next day," said Millicent.

"No news from up north?"

"No. Though I did get a box of her things in the mail today."

"From her?"

"Not exactly. Some friends sent it. She'd packed and addressed it."

"That's hopeful," said Mrs. Lacey.

It was. She would not have done it if she hadn't planned to follow it.

"Priscilla can hardly wait to meet her," she went on. "She thinks it's so romantic to be missing and have people searching for you, like something out of a story. She's got everyone in the neighborhood to promise not to wear blue until she's found, so's not to raise false hopes. Kids think of the darnedest things! But sometimes they're wiser than we are."

"Yes, sometimes they are," said Millicent. "Do thank Priscilla for me."

"I'll do that."

Wednesday. Cool and sunny. Victoria walked all day, then lost to a rebellion in the evening and bought a luscious hamburger and half-pint of milk. She carried it in torment to a little hiding place beside the road, and made herself sip half of the milk before she even tasted the hamburger, to pay herself back for spending all that money. Then she broke down and cried. She wanted it so very much, the hamburger. Something hot

136

and good. She wanted it so much it was almost like being crazy. She let go and ate it like a starving animal. She was embarrassed, all alone though she was, to have wolfed it down like that. And she felt a little sick. She lay, for a while, rolled up in a ball to ease her stomach. When the queasiness passed, she sat up in the twilight and, slowly, without slurping, finished the milk.

Another day, and another, with losing battles at suppertime. She couldn't control herself any longer. Peanut butter in the morning. Jelly at noon. And bus fare for supper. She'd get to shaking so hard by evening that she *had* to have something to eat. She knew she was losing weight. She'd picked up a bit of rope in a ditch and tied two belt loops together to hold up her jeans.

Saturday. At the end of the day, if she kept a good pace, she would be in Decorah. And she promised herself that the first thing she would do would be to find the bus station and inquire about a ticket. Iowa stretched on and on down the map and she hadn't the strength to walk that far.

She made up a chant to keep herself going: "Ticket-first, ticket-first, ticket-ticket-ticket-first." Repeated it all day. *Made* herself believe it. Go hungry if she had to, to ride on the bus. Aunt Millicent would be sure to have food in the house. Lots of food. Hot food.

"Ticket-first, ticket-first, ticket-ticket-ticket-first." Decorah was a small town and she had no trouble finding the gas station where the buses stopped.

"Dubuque? How much, you wanta know?"

She nodded, putting all her money on the counter like a little kid who couldn't add.

The man counted it out. "Just made it, if you're going one way," he said, "with a little to spare. Couldn't make a round trip by a long shot! Not running away, are you?"

"Visiting my aunt," she said.

He stamped out a ticket and pushed it across the counter to

137

her, along with seventeen cents. There was a bus in the morning that would arrive in Dubuque in the late afternoon. She needed to find a place to spend the night. There was a little bread left, a little peanut butter—she'd be all right. She had the ticket.

Victoria wandered on down the street past the Norwegian-American museum. She didn't want to go far, or get lost so near the end of her journey. It wasn't that she couldn't ask for directions, but she just didn't want to.

There was a steep hill on her left. To the right, a bridge over a sedate river, and, beyond that, a green park. She crossed the bridge and walked through the park, going on a little farther until she came to a little red house with white trim. Behind it there were large trees and shrubs. The land fell away gently to the curve of the river. It was pretty there. The house sat like a quiet friend and she was glad to be near it. She found a level spot against the trunk of a tree and sat down to make a meager supper.

There was less bread left than she'd expected, just a couple of thin ends. "Better than nothing," she told herself.

She got out the peanut butter. Not much of that left, either, but enough for the bread. A bird fluttered to the ground nearby and eyed her expectantly.

"You hungry, too?" she asked.

He hopped nearer. She broke off a bit of bread and held it out. The bird eyed it, then boldly snatched it from between her fingers. He retreated a step or two and began to eat, ignoring Victoria entirely.

Several other birds appeared and hopped about, as if waiting for their share.

"But I can't feed you all!" she said. "That's all I've got for my supper!"

"Give them your crusts and we'll see to your supper."

Victoria looked up.

"Are you very hungry?" A man stood among the trees. He had light-colored hair and warm brown eyes.

138

"Yes. Yes, I am," said Victoria.

"Then feed the birds and come with us."

Us? A child, a little girl with the same light-colored hair and merry brown eyes seemed to rise out of the earth right before her startled eyes. She was dressed entirely in earth tones that melted in with the trees and could only be seen if she moved. Bicks thought she must have stumbled on a place where elves lived. That she'd slipped from the real world into one of make-believe, for how could this girl appear like that where there had been no one a moment before?

The girl ran forward, laughing, and the man caught her up in his arms and raised her to sit on his shoulders. "Lenna has been watching," he said, "and came to tell me about you. You are alone and hungry. Give the birds your crusts. We'll find you something better." He held out his hand to her, and Bicks, knowing it was a dream, broke the bits of bread and scattered them for the birds. She picked up her shopping bag and took the offered hand.

It felt real enough, the hand. It was calloused from work and spattered with red paint. He led the way through the yard to a battered truck parked on the street in front of the house. "I have just finished the work here," he said. "Isn't it pretty?"

Bicks nodded. The red house with white trim *was* pretty, but it could have been made of gingerbread for all she knew. The truck, though, was real enough. It had been blue once but was all dents and rust now.

"My name is Jeremiah," he said, "and Lenna is my daughter. She likes to come with me here, so she can watch the birds." He reached in through the rolled-down window to open the truck door because there was no handle on the outside.

He swung Lenna from his shoulder and sat her on the seat, then lifted Victoria and set her beside his daughter. "She will speak soon," he said, "but she's shy. We may be home sooner."

He shut the door and walked around the truck. He paused to

139

look back at the house. "Yes, it's a good job." He climbed in and started the motor. It whined mournfully, all the short way to where they lived. It was a commune, he told Bicks, where everyone shared with everyone else and tried to live in harmony with the natural world.

Victoria did not know, any longer, what a commune was. She must have known once, but it had left her and she was too tired to pursue it. She only knew that there were a number of small buildings, houses perhaps, all made out of wood. There were a number of people, too, but they asked few questions, as if they expected to find, now and then, someone who was nameless and hungry.

A woman with dark hair braided into a single long braid that hung down her back gave Bicks bread and milk laced with honey. Lenna watched, with delight, while she ate it. It was not like any she had ever had before; dark, crusty, and full of flavor. "We make it," said the woman, "and find a good market for what we can't eat ourselves."

When she was done, Lenna took her hand and led her to a quiet room, where there was a row of beds made up with patchwork quilts. "Rest here for a while," she said, "then I will come with your supper." She was six, maybe seven years old, but she seemed older. Victoria couldn't find the right words and only managed to whisper her thanks.

Lenna nodded and smiled and turned back the quilt. "I'll come back," she said. Victoria fell asleep, too tired for wonder. She woke, much later, it seemed, to a gentle nudge. It was dark and there was a lamp on a table nearby, with a chimney and a little flame. It made a circle of warm, dream-like light.

Lenna sat on the floor by her bed. On a chair next to her was a steaming bowl of soup made of vegetables with cheese melting over the top. The woman with the long braid was there, smiling down on them. "Will you eat now, or shall I help you?" she asked.

140

Bicks could only stare.

"Then I will help you," the woman said. She took up the bowl and, sitting on the chair, motioned Lenna to get a pillow, which she deftly slipped under Victoria's head. It was a fat pillow that crackled and smelled of sweet hay and sunshine. A picture of golden hay ripening in the sun reeled through Bicks's mind, brightening the dark room for a moment.

The soup was delicious. Dazed by the kindness in this dream, Bicks tried to thank them. They talked quietly for a while, Bicks murmuring her answers half awake until she closed her eyes and slept again, only to wake to hear the birds singing of dawn. A gray sky opening toward morning drew the shadows from the room. Lenna was sleeping soundly in the bed next to hers. She sat up and looked around.

Though she had made no sound, Lenna was instantly awake. She smiled at Bicks, jumped out of bed, and ran, barefoot, to the window to look out at the sunrise. Victoria followed more slowly.

Veils of mist hung in the folds of the valley. The rising sun colored them with a golden light. A lazy bell was ringing and Victoria saw cows being driven to pasture. The air was fresh and green. The moment seemed fragile, but she would hold it in her mind always. She turned to see that Lenna was watching her with approval.

"Ah, Victoria, you are awake!" The young woman stood in the doorway. "Rested I see." She smiled at them. "Get your shoes and your bag and come with me. You and Lenna will eat together, and then I will take you to town to catch your bus while Lenna gathers the morning's eggs."

Bicks had not heard anyone speak her name in so long that it startled her. It sounded familiar but far away, like an echo. And it was as sharp as a knife. "When I don't answer . . ." Where *was* she?

The woman was at her side. She smoothed back her hair with

141

a gentle hand and kissed her on her forehead. "It has been a hard time for you," she said, "but it will end."

Lenna held her hand and stroked it. How did they *know*? The early sun lit the room, but it was blurred like watercolors on wet paper from the tears she could not hold back. "Say goodbye . . ."

They led her, one on each side, to her bed and sat her down. Lenna helped her with her shoes then, taking up her bag, motioned for her to rise. How did they know?

"You told us last night," said the woman, as if she had heard Bicks's unvoiced question, "of your loss and your journey. You were so tired you fell asleep in the middle of a sentence."

Victoria remembered it then. Lenna's questions, her shyness overcome by the need to know why she was all alone and had no one to take care of her.

The woman put her hand on Victoria's shoulder and guided her from the room.

There were eggs and fresh-churned butter, that good bread, and milk still warm from the cow. Bicks ate as if her supper was a far-distant memory. Lenna did not speak much through the meal, and afterward, she bolted from the room as if she'd forgotten some urgent matter. She returned and, suddenly shy again, put an object into Victoria's hand. It was a tiny bird carved out of stone. She closed Bicks's fingers around it, stood on tiptoe, kissed her on the cheek, then ran out into the sunshine.

The woman smiled after her. "Sometimes," she said, "I think that I hear the music that she walks with. But, most often, I know that I don't." She turned and, picking up a parcel wrapped in brown paper, said, "This should hold back hunger for a while." She put it in Victoria's shopping bag. "Come, I'll leave the cleaning up for later."

They bumped into town in the battered old truck. The woman, Bicks learned, was Rachel. She was Jeremiah's wife, Lenna their child. For a time she had lived in Minneapolis

142

while she went to the university, so she knew how far Victoria had come. "Don't thank me," she said. "We are glad to have helped you on your way. I ask only one thing. When you are at ease in your new home, think of us and write to tell us so. If for no one else but Lenna. She will worry. I have written the address on the wrapper. Do that and it's thanks enough." She left Bicks sitting in a sunny doorway to wait for the bus.

Sitting there, on the Sunday street, Victoria could not believe what had happened. Except that she wasn't hungry, it could have been a dream. Had she dreamed the hunger away? She reached out and touched the brown parcel in her bag. The paper was real enough and the parcel was not empty. Far from it. She put her hand into her pocket and closed her fingers around the bird. Lenna. Jeremiah. Rachel. She had no words to express what she felt. Words were such small things.

The bus was an hour away. It would be so very nice to ride after all those days of walking.

Would Aunt Millicent be home? If she wasn't, she could always wait on the porch. The afternoon services would be over when she got to Dubuque. Surely Aunt Millicent would be home by the time she climbed the steps up the face of the bluff. That much she remembered. The steps up the bluff.

The hour passed slowly. The sun was hot. The bus came. She climbed on with her shopping bag, the parcel of food riding on top. She had not said goodbye. They were not dead. She would see them again.

143

Nineteen

Millicent Purvis went to early church. Then stayed on through the second service to help in the nursery. It was something she had never done before, but she did not want to leave the place with its sense of community, and it was good to be surrounded by the soft-voiced children, who seemed to understand her need. They had offered a prayer for Victoria's safety during first services, and afterward, many had come up to her with words of encouragement and sympathy, words of comfort.

There were few passengers on the bus, most of them going only the short distance between one small town and the next. Bicks sat halfway back by a window walled in privacy by the height of the seats. She had one more thing to do before her farewell was complete. She had to read the note Mums had left for her, the twice-folded piece of paper. She took it out of Mums's purse and held it, still folded, between her hands for many long moments. Then slowly, carefully, she unfolded it as if it were a priceless document.

My dearest Victoria,

Please forgive me for not being strong enough to see you grow up. I want to so very much. It makes my heart ache to think of you being all alone in the world. But I know you will be happy with Millicent. She loves you, too, nearly as much as I do. Which is a great deal.

If, when you find this note, you are too frightened or too sad to set out for Dubuque by yourself, call her. Put a dime in the phone and tell the operator to reverse the charges. She will come to you. I know she will.

Please, dear Victoria, take care of yourself. My love will follow you even though I am not beside you. You are my life now. My joy. I am your sorrow. I beg you to forgive me.

Mums

"Oh, Mums!" Just a whisper, but her voice broke. "Oh, Mums!" The bus rolled along, eating up the miles. Victoria sat back in the seat, crying quietly. Tears made runnels down her cheeks, wet spots on her soiled shirt. "Oh, Mums."

She could have done it like that, called Aunt Millicent, but she hadn't. Someone had even told her how to do it. But it hadn't seemed possible—it was too confusing. How did you reverse the charges on a phone that didn't work unless you paid it? It seemed easier the way she'd done it, easier to walk and wear out her sorrow than to try to use the phone.

Except for the weariness and hunger, she wasn't sorry. It had been her own. Unshared. A precious farewell. No, she wasn't sorry. To share it would diminish it. It had been her own.

Forgive? There was nothing to forgive. Mums hadn't left her on purpose, it was beyond her control. Bicks remembered the smile on her face. It was a comfort to think of that. It had

145

hurt her so much during those last few days. But she must have known. She must have known the end was near. She hadn't spoken of it. She had gone away in her sleep, knowing the moment had come.

The goodbye had been said. The account paid in full. The piper had his due. There was still sorrow and tears. With time it would be less heavy. Bicks slept, her tear-stained face turned toward the window. The grief was hers, it was private.

After a time she woke, hungry, and opened the parcel. It was a lovely meal. A perfect apple, deviled eggs, more of the bread with cheese. How was it that, when she needed it most, they were there, sharing what was theirs with her, a person they didn't even know?

She carefully folded the brown paper, address in, and put it between the leaves of the little album. It was to Lenna she would write. She was Lenna's charge. Rachel had made out the address in her name. "Sometimes I think that I hear the music . . ." Bicks strained to hear it, but it was too soon. There were miles yet.

She slept again, waking only when the motion of the bus changed as it slowed from its highway speed and pulled into the outskirts of Dubuque. She felt her heart bump with anticipation. Something like excitement after the long, lonely days.

She would have to find a place to change from the clothes she'd worn for so many days—the jeans, the shirt, and the old baseball cap, and to wash up a little. She must look terribly grubby. A gas station always had rest rooms. She got off the bus and looked up and down the street. There was a man standing outside the bus depot, watching the few passengers get off. He shook his head and went back inside.

She spotted a gas station not far off and walked over to it. It was a good thing that there were paper towels in the rest room, as it would have been hard to improvise a washcloth from a roller towel. She got out the blue dress; it wasn't too wrinkled.

146

Stubs felt uncomfortable in the stiff white shirt Stace had insisted on. He'd never worn white, because you had to be so careful about it. The least smudge showed. They had been invited to Sunday-evening dinner by Mrs. Murchison and they were all dressed up. Stace looked so pretty. And she always knew what to do, Stace did. He wondered how she'd learned about the soup spoon in case there was soup, and the napkin, and what to do with two forks, and who to watch for clues. It was way too much fuss for plain eating!

Mrs. Murchison was a short, comfortable woman with white, white hair. And he soon forgot to be nervous about spoons. It was the best dinner he'd ever had in his whole life, and he wondered how Mr. Murchison kept so narrow, living with someone who could cook like that.

The phone rang . . .

Victoria chucked the last damp paper towel into the wastebasket. It was make-do. She'd only washed what showed and wished that she'd accepted the offer of a hot bath the day before. But it had seemed as if it would take too much effort and she had had no energy to spare. She bundled up the jeans and shirt and put them in the bottom of the shopping bag. They were nearly worn out. A washing would likely finish them off, but she couldn't make up her mind to throw them away. They seemed too much a part of her. After that the hat. Could you wash hats? She put the empty milk cartons in the wastebasket. Packed everything else back into the bag she carried.

She left the gas station and walked up the street toward the bluff. There were wooden stairs up the bluff face with hundreds of steps. Up and up and up. Someday she would count them all.

Halfway up she rested. Looked out across the town. The shot tower. The river beyond. It was pretty, Dubuque. She would like living here.

147

She rested again three-quarters of the way up.

How would she tell Aunt Millicent?

"She's dead. I came to live with you."

The simplest way there was.

She got to the top. Stopped to ask directions from a man picking roses in his yard. He gave her one.

Two blocks over and three down.

It was a beautiful rose. Yellow with pink edges.

Two blocks over.

"You better hurry, Charlie, or you're gonna get it!"

A boy raced past her and kept on going. Then a girl a little taller than herself. She stopped suddenly, ten paces beyond. "Keep going, Charlie! I have to talk to someone!"

She turned toward Victoria with a strange look on her face. It was as if she were seeing a ghost in the daylight.

"That's my brother, Charlie," she said. "Been dawdling on the way home and Mom's kept dinner waiting. He's in trouble, he is!"

She paused, then said shyly, hesitantly, "You're Victoria, aren't you?"

Bicks nodded, wondering how she knew.

"Oh! She'll be so glad! She'll be so glad! I'll run ahead and tell!" Priscilla gave a little leap of joy, turned, and sped off down the street. Victoria stared after her. Who? Who would be so glad? She walked on slowly. She had a pebble in her shoe.

Millicent was unlocking her front door when Priscilla Lacey clattered up the steps, out of breath.

"Miss Purvis! Oh, Miss Purvis!" she gasped. She grabbed Millicent's hand and pulled her away from the door.

"Good heavens, Priscilla! What is it?"

"She's here, Miss Purvis! She's here! Just like her school picture! She's here!"

Millicent stared at the excited girl, not believing what she'd heard. "She . . ."

148

Priscilla nodded hard.

"Victoria . . ."

"Here?"

"Just like she'd fallen out of the sky . . ."

"Oh, the good Lord be praised!"

"There! See?" Priscilla pointed up the street.

Through her tears, Millicent could see a little figure walking toward her. A little figure in a blue dress.

Everything else receded. She saw only the little girl. She didn't hear Priscilla shouting for joy. Calling to her family to come see. She didn't see the steps, stumbled, and nearly fell. She walked toward Victoria in a daze, arms outstretched.

Like Daddy, Bicks thought. She looks like Daddy. She hadn't remembered that. For a second she thought she saw them coming up behind her, hand in hand, her daddy and Mums. But only for a second; then she was in Aunt Millicent's arms, falling down, down.

For a while she lost track of things. She was in a familiar house and didn't know how she got there. There was a confusion of voices and the phone ringing, ringing. Sometimes far away, sometimes near.

She remembered asking if she could have a bath and a strange woman taking her upstairs to the bathroom.

"Who are you?" Bicks asked.

"I'm Mrs. Lacey," she said. "I've been watching for you all week while Millicent was at work."

"You're somebody's mother," said Bicks.

Mrs. Lacey smiled. "Yes, I am. Priscilla. She's my oldest. She's the one that spotted you coming down the street. She's a bit rattled now by all the excitement. But you'll like her, I'm sure, once she settles down."

Aunt Millicent came in with some fancy pajamas for her to put on. Brand-new. And a pretty bathrobe with lace on it.

Then there was Priscilla and Charlie. In and out. Pris said

149

the baby threw up and wouldn't go to sleep. Mrs. Lacey left with her. Mr. Lacey came in with someone from the bus depot. Bicks had seen him before, standing outside when the bus came in. He was glad to meet her. Glad to know she was home at last. Home. Such a wonderful word.

The phone kept ringing. People calling to say how very glad they were. Before the news got out, Aunt Millicent had placed a call to Minneapolis. Mr. Murchison. Who was he? The man at the funeral home. He'd gone out every morning to wait by the grave, thinking she would come back. And he'd bought more flowers, grand flowers, when hers had faded. Her best wish had been lilacs in a pickle jar once a year. She cried then, and Aunt Millicent had taken her in her arms and comforted her.

Pris gave her a doll. One of her very own. She held it gingerly, not knowing what to say.

"It's a doll," said Priscilla, "for you to keep."

"A doll?"

"You mean you've never had one?"

"Yes. Once. Somewhere else. I can't take your doll. Then you won't have one."

"But I've got other dolls. I want you to have it."

"All right," said Bicks. She stared at Pris as if she were a being from another planet. A doll. She held it close to her. "Thank you," she said at last. "I'll take good care of it."

Pris went home with a promise to come back in the morning. The phone had stopped ringing and quiet settled over the house. Aunt Millicent carried Victoria to bed. Sunset filled the room with flame. She tucked her in, then opened the window to an evening breeze that smelled, faintly, of roses. She did not speak, it was not necessary, but sat on the edge of the bed, holding her niece's hand.

The light faded. The day was over and night had come. Victoria was home.